MW00783440

JEKKA WILDE

JACK OF DIAMONDS

THE WICKED BOYS OF WONDERLAND

BOOK THREE

Copyright © 2023 Jekka Wilde

All rights reserved.

Cover design by Wilde & Free

This is a work of fiction. Names, characters, businesses, coffee shops, organizations, places, events, and incidents either are the products of the author's imagination or are used fictitiously. Any resemblance to actual monster cocks, vampire cocks, demon cocks, fae cocks, events, locales, organizations, or persons, living or dead, is entirely coincidental.

ISBN: 978-1-964291-02-4

CONTENTS

CHAPTER
ONE

ALICE

Frost and starlight streamed down from the unearthly swirls of color above, bathing the pale stone walls of the White Queen's castle in ethereal light. Everything was made of glittering ice and shimmering crystals that cast rainbows along the hallways and floors.

We were in the Kingdom of Diamonds and Ice.

We were safe.

For now.

As we entered a grand atrium, majestic columns rose around us, adorned with intricate carvings of centaurs and fae and other mythical creatures. A giant crystal fountain stood at the heart of the room, spewing enchanted water that formed an elaborate sculpture of intertwined dragons and vines.

The sheer wonder and beauty of our surroundings should've left me in awe, but I didn't have time to admire the view.

Ransom was suffering.

Maybe even dying.

1

"We're almost there," Jack murmured as he led me, Hatter, Chess, and Callister around yet another corner.

"You said that five minutes ago!" I snapped at him. "How big is this fucking castle?"

Jack slowly glanced over his shoulder and gave me a sharp look with his blood-red eyes, but he said nothing. If he was trying to scare me, it wasn't working.

I was already scared.

The last thing I cared about was manners.

Ransom's life hung in the balance, and I'd be damned if I was going to stand by and just let him die.

My gaze darted down to where he lay on the floating stretcher. He was curled up on one side, enveloped almost entirely by his torn and bloody wings. They clung to his body like wet, black canvas, tattered like a pirate's flag after a battle at sea. Slimy black blood oozed from his countless injuries, dripping and pooling onto the white fabric stretcher that carried his body.

"Hold on, my king," I reassured him between his shudders of pain. "We're almost there."

He grimaced and let out a groan, then peered up at me.

"Alice . . ."

"I'm right here. I'm not going anywhere."

I desperately wanted to touch him, to comfort him, to even just hold his hand, but Jack had warned me against coming into contact with his poisoned blood.

Unfortunately, Ransom was covered in it.

All I could do was walk alongside his floating stretcher in our search for the White Queen.

A pair of women emerged from a side corridor, one of them dressed in simple robes and furiously scribbling notes. The other one in the stunning white dress and matching crown was busy dictating a message.

They both stopped in their tracks the moment they saw our bedraggled entourage headed their way. The woman in white took one look at the body on the floating stretcher and her eyes widened.

"Ransom!" she gasped at the sight of him. Her concern was genuine, and I felt a warmth spread within me, knowing that she cared for him as much as I did. "What's happened?"

"He's been shot by poisoned arrows, Your Majesty," Jack informed her. The woman's mouth pursed, her lips tight and drawn.

"I take it this is my sister's doing?"

"It is, unfortunately."

"Bring him this way."

The woman—the White Queen, I realized—stormed towards a set of double doors and flung them wide open.

We followed her into a large room filled with shelves upon shelves of glass bottles and jars and boxes of medical supplies. A large white stone exam table stood in the center of the room, and I watched

Hatter and Chess guide the stretcher above it before gently lowering Ransom into place.

I didn't know why the exam table had a wide juice canal carved all the way around it until thick, sticky black blood trickled down the sides of Ransom's body. A hissing sound rose up from tiny spirals of steam as the hot blood hit the icy cold stone. Then it seeped into the groove before traveling to the end near his feet, where it trickled like molasses into a metal bucket.

The White Queen snapped her fingers. A white leather apron materialized and wrapped around her dress while long white gloves covered her hands up past her elbows. Eight men and women in white robes appeared, and immediately conjured matching aprons and gloves.

"We must act quickly to counteract the black magic poisoning these wounds," she said to her team. She stepped over to Ransom's side, gently examining the jagged tears in his wing to assess the damage. Her brow creased as she registered the extent of his wounds. The holes were melting away the flesh right before our eyes, to the point that I could see the queen through them. With a determined nod, she set down Ransom's wing and turned to her attendants, then began issuing crisp orders to them.

"Prepare a poultice of moonflower elixir, Tears of the Fae, and six bundles of healing herbs," she instructed one of the women, her voice both gentle and commanding. She turned to the other two women. "And I need you to fetch my stores of dragon's blood resin and crushed opal. We're going to need everything I have."

While her assistants hurried off to collect the supplies, she pointed at the three men.

"Turn him onto his belly. Mind the horns. We'll need a dedicated team for each of his wings if we're going to have any chance of saving them."

They nodded, their faces grim with determination.

While the men maneuvered Ransom into position, the White Queen twisted a silver handled faucet and began filling a large basin with water.

"Is anyone else injured?"

I looked around at each of my wicked boys. Hatter and Callister shook their heads, but Chess reluctantly held out his arm for inspection. More of the black ooze was dripping down his wrist, staining the white cuff of his shirt.

"They shot through my paw," he admitted. "But it can wait. Ransom needs your full attention."

The White Queen shook her head while pouring half a bottle of milky white fluid into the basin of water.

"If we don't treat your hand now, the poison will spread through the rest of your body. Come here so I can wash it out. One of my assistants will apply a poultice and bandage it for you."

She took Chess's hand and poured a ladle full of the milky white water over it. A loud hiss filled my ears and it took me a moment to register that it wasn't coming from the hot blood hitting the cold stone. My

5

heart clenched when I realized the source of the sound.

It was coming from my fierce Cheshire Cat.

If the simple act of washing out a single wound from an arrow had caused him that much pain, what would it do to Ransom, when he had dozens of injuries?

He'd be in agony.

As if reading my thoughts, the White Queen looked up at me.

"You should leave now."

"Let me stay with him. Please," I insisted. "He risked his life to save us!"

She shook her head of long, dark purple coils that seemed to defy gravity. Although her face was kind, her voice was firm.

"The best way to repay his sacrifice is to give me and my apprentices enough room to work. Chess can keep him company."

"Take good care of him," I choked out, my voice barely above a whisper.

One of the apprentices turned to me, offering a reassuring smile. "Don't worry. Queen Amari has healed far worse."

I bit my lip, watching as the men carefully extended each of Ransom's battered wings onto a pair of long, narrow tables. His face was pale beneath the blood, and his eyes squeezed shut from the excruciating pain.

"Shuttlecocks and teapots . . . " Hatter breathed

as he placed a hand on my lower back. "I've seen lace with less holes in it."

His comment wasn't much of an exaggeration.

My heart sank as I took one last look at the poison burning holes through Ransom's flesh like acid.

"Do you really think he'll be alright?"

"He can't get much worse," Callister muttered under his breath.

"I'll send word once he's stable," said the White Queen. "Now please, let us work. Jacques will show you to your rooms. I'm glad you're here, Alice. I'm sure we'll get acquainted soon."

I didn't remember Callister, Hatter, and I being ushered out of the room. My mind was completely numb as we walked down a series of halls that all looked the same—shimmering blurs of icy blue and white.

My chest felt hollow and empty, yet aching with the image of Ransom's motionless form lying face-down on the exam table . . . his leathery, feathery wings outstretched like a broken bird.

He had to be alright.

He just *had* to.

"Alice? Where are you going?"

"Huh?"

I blinked in confusion at the unfamiliar voice, then glanced around.

Jack was standing beside a door, watching me with an unreadable expression. Was he suspicious? Curious? Insulted? Annoyed?

I had a feeling that even if I asked, he wouldn't tell me.

"This is your room."

Still numb with worry for Ransom, I returned to Jack's side just as he grasped the handle and pushed against the door. It slowly drifted open, revealing a breathtaking scene straight out of a fairy tale.

White stone walls were covered with framed paintings of surreal creatures of Wonderland. Cut crystal windows edged with frost offered a twilight view of the enchanting icy landscape outside. Above me, the ceiling seemed to be made of twinkling stars that cast an ethereal blue light throughout most of the room.

A roaring fireplace crackled at one end, providing warmth that contrasted with the cold beauty of the crystal palace. The bed was covered in multiple thick and cozy white blankets, practically begging me to dive in and bury myself away from the day's turmoil.

I stepped into my room, seeing that I had my own private bathroom with a huge tub beneath an even bigger window. A stack of fluffy white towels sat on a table beside it.

A sudden shadow shot past me. To my surprise, Jack was standing in the middle of the room. Broad shoulders covered in black armor cut a sharp outline against the backdrop of soft white blankets and pillows.

I hadn't seen him take a step past me, yet there he was. The swirl of his cloak was the only clue that he'd moved from the doorway to where he now stood.

"H—how did you do that?" I stammered.

The firelight gleamed against the rippled breast-plate covering his chest, his gorgeous face, and his long platinum hair.

Then his red eyes flicked over to me.

"I move quickly. Faster than your human eyes can comprehend."

I yelped as he suddenly appeared right in front of me, staring deep into my eyes, holding my gaze as if by some kind of magical power.

Either that, or he was just fine as hell and I couldn't force myself to look away.

The light from the fireplace highlighted every sharp angle of his facial bone structure, every soft curve of his lips, and the shadows cast by his long, dark eyelashes.

He looked me up and down, not bothering to mask his disappointed frown.

I wasn't used to men looking at me like that—with complete disdain.

"You are here to learn how to use the Vorpal Sword. I expect your full cooperation. It's going to be a monumental task for me to train you to my satis-faction."

Unable to speak, all I could do was nod.

Despite the blazing fire nearby, his scentless breath fell on my face like a soft, cool breeze. I couldn't help wondering what he meant by training me to his satisfaction.

Jack didn't strike me as someone who was easy to please.

"The path to becoming a formidable warrior begins with discipline, unwavering dedication, and a relentless pursuit of excellence. Give yourself fully to me, and I will forge you like the finest of blades."

I noticed the door was still open. Why the fuck was Jack still in my room? I pulled the collar of my white fur coat tight around my neck and took a step away from the vampire.

"What exactly do you mean that I have to give myself to you?"

"I mean that you're not here for social reasons. Nor are you here for pleasure. You're here to *work*," came his cool, arrogant reply. "Whatever loyalty you harbor for Ransom and the others must come *after* your obligation to me. Disobey, and I will make your existence a living hell."

He took another step towards me, closing the gap between us before narrowing his cold gaze at me.

"Every moment you spend in the White Queen's court will be spent in training. When eat, you will think of nothing but what I teach you. When you sleep, you will dream of nothing but what you've learned. Do you understand?"

"Sounds like a full-immersion program," I blurted without thinking.

"Oh, it is," he replied, his face softening with a

faint, yet sadistic grin. "And without my help, you will drown."

My eyes flew open.

"The fuck? I'm pretty sure you need me more than I need you."

I watched as Jack's pupils dilated until his red irises were nearly all black. He leaned down just enough for his pale hair to spill down his armored shoulders.

His powerful, massive, armored shoulders.

I forgot all about my shitty manners and remembered I was standing in front of a deadly killer.

"Tomorrow will be a very long day for you, Alice, so I suggest you get some rest. We will meet outside the Great Hall. Your training begins at dawn." He blinked, and his eyes went back to normal. They narrowed as if to scold me for something I hadn't yet done.

Finally, Jack stood up straight, then turned on his heel and headed for the door.

"Lesson number one—don't be late."

CHAPTER

TWO

ALICE

The second Jack left my room, I slammed the door
shut and locked it. I leaned back against the heavy
oak slab and took a deep breath.

I dove into the cloud-like softness of my bed and
pulled the fluffy blankets up to my chin. The light
from the fire made the pale, shimmering walls look
alive with constant movement.

I didn't realize that I'd fallen asleep until I felt the
gentle sensation of fingers on my scalp, playing with
my hair. My eyes fluttered open to see Chess, his
intense gaze locked onto me.

Above him, the sparkling beauty of an enchanted
night sky glimmered and twinkled. Hot coals in the
fireplace cast the pale walls in soft, warm, orange
light.

"Ah, you're awake," Chess murmured, his voice
like velvet against my ears. I couldn't tell if he'd come
with good news . . .

Or with bad.

"How's Ransom?" I asked groggily, rubbing sleep from my eyes.

"He's alive," he explained, his fingers continuing their soothing dance along my scalp. "Queen Amari and her apprentices have been working on him all night. They're still not done drawing out all the poison, but they're close. It'll take some time for him to fully recover."

My chest tightened at the memory of Ransom's battered body, how his cocky, commanding presence had crumbled under the weight of his wounds. I tried to imagine what he must be going through. The pain was so foreign and yet so real in my heart.

"Did they have to amputate his wings?" I asked, worry lacing my voice.

Chess shook his head.

"Amari is doing everything she can to avoid it. She's a skilled healer, Alice. If anyone can bring him back from the brink, it's her. Look at my hand." He held it up, flexing his fingers with ease. "You'd never know that I'd been wounded mere hours ago."

I let out a shaky breath, trying to find comfort in his words.

Maybe Ransom would be okay after all.

Maybe this nightmare could still have a happy ending.

But the nagging doubt in the back of my mind refused to be silenced.

"Thanks for letting me know, Chess," I whispered, reaching for his healed hand and intertwining our fingers. His touch was warm and reassuring, a lifeline amidst the cold uncertainty that surrounded us.

"Anything for you." His lips curved into a tender smile as he curled his other arm around my back, leaned down, then pressed a soft kiss to my forehead.

For a fleeting moment, I allowed myself to be swept away by the simple pleasure of his touch, the way it ignited a fire within me that burned so brightly it chased away the darkness.

But as I stared into his eyes, full of sincere devotion, I couldn't help but wonder if I truly deserved him. If I was worthy of the affection he so freely offered. It was impossible to ignore the complexities of my relationship with him . . . with his friends.

Chess was enigmatic and seductive. Ransom was demanding and dangerous. Hatter was obscene and insane, and even Callister evoked a love-hate attraction inside of me. They all had their secrets, their motives, and yet, I was completely drawn to each of them for different reasons.

In this strange, dream-like world, I found myself tangled in a web of desire with my Wicked Boys of Wonderland.

"Chess," I began hesitantly, unsure of how to voice my concerns. "I'm sorry I fucked Callister and Ransom and Hatter right after you left. I didn't plan on it, but—"

"Shhh . . . " With a soft Cheshire grin, he pressed

a finger to my lips. "I'd have done the same thing if I'd been in their position. Truth be told, I'm glad you fucked Callister. His mood has been greatly improved ever since you did."

"I'm sorry if I made you jealous."

"How could I be jealous?" he purred. "They're like brothers to me, Alice." His fingers left my lips and began tracing along my jaw, my neck, then my collarbone. "We know how to share . . . to take turns."

A soft, warm throb awakened my core.

"That's good to know," I whispered, my voice barely audible.

Chess revealed a soft smile as he delicately grazed the tips of his fingers over my exposed skin, causing goosebumps to form in their wake. His fingers traveled down the length of my arm before slipping under the covers, where he discovered that I was naked underneath.

His eyes took on a wicked gleam.

I knew *exactly* what that look meant.

"Such a lovely surprise," he murmured, his voice low and filled with desire as he pushed away the blankets. I shivered at the sudden sensation of cool air against my skin. Then I moaned as he slowly began teasing my nipples with his fingertips. They made gentle circles around them before he pinched them between his thumb and forefinger.

He dipped his head until he'd sucked one of my tits into his mouth. A gasp escaped me as he softly nibbled until my nipple was hard against his tongue. A rush of arousal coursed through my body, making

16

me ache for Chess in ways I hadn't anticipated. I could feel the slick wetness pooling on the other side of my pussy lips.

"Oh, you delightful girl," Chess murmured as he looked up at me. "I can smell your delicious cunt."

The heat of his touch sent a jolt of pleasure coursing through me, and I couldn't help but moan in response.

"You feel so good . . . but I'm too tired to fuck," I gasped, my body arching towards him as he continued to torment my sensitive nubs.

"You're beyond tired. You're exhausted," Chess soothed, leaning down to press a gentle kiss to my lips while massaging my tits. "Why don't you lie back and relax, and let me do all the fucking? All you have to do is say the word."

I looked up at him through heavy-lidded eyes.

"Wouldn't that make me lazy?"

"Lazy? That's not an adjective I'd use when describing you." He gazed into my eyes, a devilish grin playing on his lips. "However, if you're too tired to let me lick you and suck you, or allow my tongue to fuck you, then I will leave and let you rest."

My body trembled, torn between exhaustion and my mounting desire. I knew exactly what that tongue was capable of. Turning down such a generous offer bordered on sacrilegious.

"No! Don't go," I said, biting my lip in antic-ipation.

"I don't know . . . " he taunted, pulling away from

me. "Are you sure you have the energy for such . . . *vigorous* activities?"

"Yeah, I'm sure," I panted, my weak fingers tangling in his hair as I unsuccessfully tried to pull him closer. "I want you. I *need* you, Chess. Now."

Cheshire nodded, grinning wider.

"Very well," he agreed after a moment's hesitation, his eyes darkening with desire as they swept over my flushed face. "You just lie back and let me do all the work. Can you do that for me?"

"Hell yeah," I breathed, my heart pounding in anticipation as I nodded. "You can do anything you want to me."

"You can count on it, darling," Chess replied with a wicked grin. His eyes darkened with lust, and while his skilled fingers continued teasing my nipples, I found my thoughts drifting back to our previous encounters, my body growing hotter by the second. Chess had a way of making me feel both vulnerable and powerful at the same time, and I craved more of that intoxicating sensation.

His clothes melted away, revealing hard, sleek muscles that were backlit with deep orange fire from the hearth. Broad shoulders made for prowling. Powerful legs made for running. Abs that would rock and thrust against me all night long.

But it was his huge, freakishly shaped cock that made me shudder. Of all my wicked boys, his was the biggest. The thickest. I'd always thought of myself as a bit of a size queen, but this demon dick gave me pause.

No wonder Chess needed that magical tentacle tongue.

Foreplay wasn't an option for him.

It was mandatory.

With the lightest touch, his fingernails clawed against my throat and raked through my hair, demonstrating their delicious torture as he prepared to take me to new heights of pleasure.

As the first tendrils of ecstasy began to unfurl within me, I knew that no matter how exhausted I was, there was no denying the magnetic pull between us. The connection we shared was undeniable, a force more powerful than any I had ever known.

As Chess continued to arouse me with his expert touch, my thoughts drifted to the complicated relationship I had with each one of my wicked boys. I couldn't help but wonder what the future held for us, especially given that I had feelings for all of them.

I couldn't pick just one.

But for now, all that mattered was the feel of the Cheshire Cat's caress on my skin, the sound of his voice whispering sweet nothings in my ear, and the knowledge that, at least for this moment, we were exactly where we were meant to be.

"Relax your mind, Alice," he whispered into my ear as he effortlessly crawled on top of me. His voice was low and seductive. The heat of his body enveloped me as he nestled between my thighs. His breath was hot and tantalizing against the sensitive skin there.

"Now relax your body, and let me take care of

you," he purred. He positioned his mouth over my mound, then pressed a tender kiss to the inside of my thigh before lowering his lips closer to my slick, swollen center.

His demon tongue flicked out, teasing me, tracing the outline of my folds, making me shiver in anticipation. I couldn't help but let out a soft moan as his skilled tongue began to explore me, dancing over my clit and dipping into my wetness with sensual strokes.

"Chess . . . oh, fuck, yes . . . " I whimpered as my hips bucked impatiently up and down against his face.

I was met with a broad, fat, hot, wet tongue. Its only purpose was for me to enjoy it . . .

So enjoy it I did.

My hips rolled up and down, riding his face like a slip & slide. I gasped, my back arching off the bed as pleasure surged through me.

His mouth closed around my cunt, sucking gently on my clit. I let out a hiss, then sank my fingers in his dark hair, curling them around the back of his head as I started fucking his face harder.

My arousal built to dizzying heights while he continued to work me mercilessly. He kept alternating between slow, languid licks and quick, sharp flicks that sent jolts of electricity coursing through me.

Then his demon tongue pushed past my slippery pussy lips. It instantly began to change shape, growing thicker and longer by the second, morphing into a thick, wet tentacle that gently filled and stretched my inner walls.

Suddenly he stopped.

I looked up to see him frowning slightly while sucking on something in his mouth. He spit a tiny gold object into his hand, staring at it in confusion. Then he held it out so we both could see exactly what it was.

My heart nearly stopped beating.

"Alice? Why is Ransom's Ring of Temptation hidden inside your cunt? I thought the Red Queen had stolen it from him."

"She did . . . " I trembled as my heart leapt in disbelief. Amidst the Red Queen's attack on us back at the Rabbit Hole and then Ransom getting hurt, I'd forgotten all about what had triggered the shitshow to begin with.

"Remember how we all came up with a plan for me and Ransom to lure the Red Queen up to his room?"

"I remember," Chess nodded. "The plan was for Ransom to seduce the queen and you were supposed to cut off her head with the Vorpal Sword."

A twinge of shame rattled me at remembering how my failure had almost cost Ransom his life.

But I hadn't completely failed.

Thanks to my spectacular pussy (and doing kegels regularly), I had the Ring of Temptation.

"Well, Ransom had taken off my collar by then, so I was able to use my imagination again," I started to explain. "The Red Queen started fingering me,

21

and I imagined my pussy clamping down on her as tight as possible. It was my only chance, so I took it."

"How marvelous . . . " Chess snickered as he studied the ring even closer. Then his green eyes darted over to me. "Your tight, slippery cunt stole the ring right off Roxanne's finger. You might not have killed her, but you've dealt quite a blow to her power over others."

"I have?"

Chess nodded, then carefully set the ring on the nearby nightstand.

"Oh yes. The Ring of Temptation carries the power of seduction. It makes those around you unlikely to oppose you. This ring is a large reason why so many of the Red Queen's subjects are unable to defy her or stand up against her. Now that she's lost this ring, and that power, her subjects and her soldiers aren't going to be quite as obedient."

I felt a deep burst of pride that my efforts had paid off so well. Chess let out a deep, satisfied purr, then grasped my thighs once more.

"You deserve to be rewarded . . . again . . . and again . . . and again . . . "

His hot, wet tentacle tongue flicked at my clit, then crammed its long girth back inside me.

"Chess . . . oh holy shit . . . " I moaned, gripping the sheets tightly as his tongue fluttered and rippled and flexed, filling my pussy like a massive prehensile cock. He moved it slowly at first, teasing me with shallow, deliberate strokes. The sensation made me feel as if every nerve ending inside me was on fire.

22

The Cheshire Cat was fucking me with his demon tentacle cock-tongue, making me melt into his mouth.

I could feel my arousal building, my pussy clenching around Chess's talented demon tongue, my juices spreading all over his face. He quickened his pace, plunging deeper and deeper into me, each thrust harder, thicker than the last. My breath came in ragged gasps as I felt myself approaching the edge, my entire body trembling with need.

When he pulled his organ out of me, I practically sobbed.

"No . . . don't stop!" I begged, my nails digging into my thighs as I tried to hold onto some semblance of control. But the pleasure was too much, too all-consuming, and I knew that I wouldn't be able to resist it for much longer.

"Patience, darling," Chess murmured, his fingers sliding down to explore the slick folds of my pussy. He teased my entrance before dipping two fingers inside, curling them in a come-hither motion that had me writhing in ecstasy.

"Tell me how it feels when the cat plays with your pussy," he purred from between my wet thighs. His voice was thick with desire as he paused to look up at me. The sight of him kneeling before me, his green eyes dark with lust and his lips glistening with my juices, nearly made me come right then and there.

"It's . . . incredible," I managed to gasp out, my hips involuntarily arching towards him, seeking more of his intoxicating touch.

"Be more specific," he growled.

I panted, racking my brain for the right words to describe the indescribable.

"It's squishy, but firm. It's so soothing, even though it's hot," I breathed. "And I love the way it gets thicker and thicker and presses against me. It makes me feel so . . . so . . . "

"Yes? I'm listening." His brilliant green eyes lit up, urging me to go on.

"You make me feel so full, and I love it." I locked my eyes onto his. "Chess . . . I want you inside me. I want you to fill every last inch of me!"

"Are you sure, Alice?" he asked, raising an eyebrow suggestively as he looked down at my quivering body. "Because if I fuck you with my cock, I'm not going to stop until I've drained myself into you . . . until I've exhausted every last drop of my magic. We're safe here, so I can afford to indulge . . . "

His eyes narrowed as he gazed down at my shiny, slick pussy. Then his gaze flicked up to my own.

The primal gleam they suddenly held was impossible to ignore.

"I went easy on you the last time. If I fuck you tonight, I'm going to give it to you harder than ever. I'm going to mount you and ride you long and hard . . . right into oblivion." He used his fingers to comb his dark hair out of his gorgeous face. "You've seen my true form. I make no promise of how gentle I'll be."

"I don't care—now c'mon and fuck me already!" I demanded breathlessly. I glared at the massive

24

demon cock he was withholding from me, then shot him an expectant look.

Get inside, you fucking tease!

That Cheshire grin spread across his face, and I remembered he could read my thoughts. But I wasn't about to give in to his game of cat and mouse.

Grabbing a pillow, I shoved it under my ass, then tilted my hips up and spread my legs wider. I imagined the firelight reflecting off my slick, wet pussy lips. I knew what he wanted more than anything else in that moment—to sink that fat demon dick inside and blast me full of cum.

"Here, kitty, kitty . . . " I teased with a smirk. "Don't let all this fresh cream go to waste."

Chess pounced on me without warning, unfurling his tongue before plunging it into my slit. He let out a satisfied growl as the wet muscle flexed and thickened inside me, pumping and thrusting as he hungrily drank me in.

The silky, yet slightly rough texture had me whimpering and thrashing against the pillow under my hips, against the mattress. Warm, wet saliva mixed with my juices and trickled down the crack in my ass.

He pulled his tongue out of me, making me howl with indignation.

"You think you outsmarted me, but you're mine now . . . " he declared with a wicked grin. "Mine to fuck however I please."

His fingers slipped into my dripping cunt with

sinful ease, pumping and gliding while his thumb made little circles around my swollen clit.

"Fuck, Chess," I moaned, my mind spinning with the dual sensations of his thumb on my clit and his fingers working me. He crooked his fingers, expertly massaging that secret spot inside me that made stars burst behind my eyes.

Meanwhile, his demon tentacle tongue unfurled again. This time he licked one long, slow, languid trail after another up and down my crack, bathing my ass in hot, wet euphoria.

It teased the tight ring of muscle at my back entrance, swirling around, building pressure.

I couldn't make words.

All I could do was spread for him.

Give him everything he wanted . . . and more.

The tip of his tongue pressed into me with ease, and I let out a husky groan, unable to form a coherent thought beyond the desperate need for more of him.

His hot, greedy, demanding, wet muscle pulsed and thrust deep into my channel, and I couldn't help but gasp at the deliciously illicit sensation. Chess continued to stretch and fill me with his tongue and fingers, pushing me closer and closer to the edge with every inhuman caress.

"Chess, I'm . . . I'm gonna come!" I cried out, shamelessly begging for him to push me over the edge.

The combination of his tongue and fingers sent waves of filthy pleasure racing through me, and I knew that it wouldn't take much more to bring me to climax. I panted, feeling the pressure within me build to an almost unbearable intensity.

I'd never been tongue-fucked in the ass by a demon . . . but it felt like my ass was made for it.

As if giving me permission, Chess hummed in approval, his voice low and seductive as he increased the tempo of his fingers and tongue.

The vibrations of his humming traveled through his tongue, anchoring in my ass while making me come apart in his arms. He sent me careening over the edge, my orgasm crashing through me with a force that left me shaking and breathless.

"Chess, please . . . fuck me!" I howled while my ass clenched down on his tongue. My voice was a gasping groan as my body trembled in the throes of euphoria. My heart raced, and I could feel the ache between my legs growing more desperate with every passing second.

His fingers in my pussy were a mediocre place-holder for what I really wanted.

I watched him slip his long tentacle tongue out of my ass and roll it back into his mouth.

"Are you sure, Alice?" Chess asked softly, his eyes darkening with desire but still shining with genuine concern for my well-being. "I don't want to push you too far."

"For fuck's sake, just gimme your fucking cock!" I yelled at him, tilting my hips up to meet him. My insatiable need to be filled consumed me, and I knew that only Chess could satiate my carnal desires.

"I love hearing you beg for it," Chess murmured,

a wicked grin spreading across his face. He moved over me, positioning himself between my spread thighs, and took hold of his massive, thick cock, teasing the fat head against my dripping wet entrance. As he pushed forward, I felt simultaneously stretched wide and soothed.

Once he'd worked his full length into me, I whimpered at the sensation of the soft nubs and bumps above his enormous cock. They rubbed against my clit with every breath he took, sending shivers of delight through my core, through my skin, throughout my entire body.

"Fuck, that feels so good," I moaned, my nails digging into his broad shoulders as he began to thrust deeper inside me. I was coming down from my orgasm, but I knew with him that another one was right around the corner.

"Does it now?" Chess asked with a smirk, his pace quickening as he watched the pleasure dance across my face.

"Fuck, yeah it does!" I gasped, lost in the sensations that threatened to overwhelm me. I could feel my walls stretching to accommodate his size, and those soft, slick nubs slipping and sliding over my clit with every movement he made. The pressure building within me was almost unbearable.

"You're so tight, Alice," he groaned, his voice strained with effort and desire. "So slippery and hot. No wonder this cunt of yours was able to grab a ring right off the Red Queen's finger. I can feel you squeezing me . . . tugging me. You were made for this. Made for fucking me."

As Chess relentlessly pumped his thick cock into me, filling me to the brim, I felt a new kind of pleasure building. His fingers slipped around my body, seeking out the entrance to my ass. I shuddered in delight as he began to finger fuck me there, simultaneously driving his demon cock deeper into my pussy.

"Holy fuck, Chess," I moaned, my body quivering with every thrust and grind and intrusion. The extra stimulation sent me into orgasmic overdrive, and I found myself squeezing . . . bucking . . . doing everything I could to increase the friction.

"I lied to you, Alice," he panted, his eyes filled with pure, primal lust. "I was more than jealous when I realized that you'd fucked Hatter *and* Ransom *and* Callister while I was fetching the Vorpal Sword from Hell. I was fucking *incensed*! But it just made me want to claim you even more."

His confession only fueled the fire within me, and I could feel the looming power of my next orgasm building.

"You want to claim me?" I asked breathlessly, my chest heaving from both the physical exertion and the emotional impact of his words.

"More than anything," he growled, his gaze locked onto mine. "I want to fill your tight little pussy with my cum. I want it so full of my demon seed that you're brimming over with it. I want to breed you one day, and bind you to me forever."

The raw intensity in his voice, combined with the relentless pounding of his cock inside me, pushed me over the edge once more. I lifted my hips and stared into his very soul.

"Breed me now, Chess!" I demanded. "Fill me up with everything you've got!"

"Oh, fuck . . . Alice!" he roared, his hips slamming against me, pinning me down on the bed. With one final, brutal thrust, he sank deep into my core, releasing a torrent of hot cum that flooded my depths.

I imagined it spilling deep into my body, imagined my greedy pussy gobbling up every last drop, sucking his balls dry like his cock was a fountain of pleasure. He moaned my name again, all but crying in my ear as his thickness convulsed and twitched inside me.

Every shudder of his body made the nubs vibrate against my clit, and the sensation of him pinning me down and coming inside of me with his wet fingers still buried in my ass was too much.

I closed my eyes and let myself go.

With a final, desperate cry, I surrendered to the waves of ecstasy that crashed over me. As my inner walls constricted around his length, I drew my legs up and wrapped them around him. I wanted to be drenched in every fucking drop of his cum.

"I'm not finished!" he snarled, revealing more than a hint of the demonic beast that occupied his body.

"Give me everything!" I panted, clutching him against my body.

His demon cock swelled again, stretching me
until it hurt, but I refused to let go. Another wave of
molten heat poured into me, and I knew he was
coming inside me again. His hips flexed and curled as
he thrusted deep. Then he held me down, pinning
me into the mattress, letting his cock pulse and throb
and fill me until there was nothing more to give.

THREE

ALICE

Gooey, sticky warmth surrounded me as I opened my eyes to the bright yellow light of mid-morning flooding my white room. I rolled onto my side, still feeling the delicious ache from my all-night fuckfest with Chess. The Cheshire Cat demon was sleeping next to me, purring against my neck, his arm draped over my waist.

Chess had ridden me hard . . . so fucking hard, and drenched me in so much cum that there was no way in hell I was leaving this room without taking a shower.

The memory of Jack standing in the middle of this room last night seemed like a dream, and I found myself longing to believe it. There weren't any clocks in my room, but I knew it was well after dawn. I gently pushed away Chess's arm from my waist. His fingers spread out like claws, pulling my ass against his hips.

"I have to get up," I grumbled, squirming like a

mouse caught in his grasp. "I'm late for training with Jack."

Chess yawned, stretching out across my silken sheets like a giant feline. "Don't worry, darling. The White Knight should know better than to expect punctuality from you. After all . . . " His hand slid between my sticky thighs, his clever fingers awakening my arousal. "You're already years and years behind schedule. What's another hour . . . or five?"

I pushed his hand away, then twisted around to face him, shooting him a skeptical glance.

It was met with a classic Cheshire Cat grin playing on his lips, and I knew exactly what sinful thoughts were running through his head.

"No."

Chess's green eyes fluttered in mock innocence.

"I didn't say anything."

"You didn't have to," I smirked.

"There's plenty of time for lessons." Chess argued, nuzzling my neck. Suddenly he pounced on me, pinning me beneath him. I groaned at the primal, satisfying sensation of his weight on me. He knew *exactly* how to touch me, and I couldn't help but crave more.

"Why don't we continue where we left off last night?" he purred in triumph.

I bit my lip, desire warring with duty. As much as I wanted to stay in bed with Chess, I knew I wasn't here on vacation.

Wonderland needed me.

The White Knight was waiting for me.

And Ransom would want his magic ring as soon as possible.

"I can't, Chess," I said from underneath him. "I'm already late, and I still need to take a shower." I gave him a gentle pat on the ass. He politely nodded, then crawled off of me and out of the bed.

"You don't need to waste more precious time bathing."

"Yeah, I do," I said, glancing down at the dried sweat and cum all over my skin.

"You're in Wonderland, Alice." He grinned before tapping his temple. "Use your imagination to get what you want." He snapped his fingers, and I watched his dirty hair magically fall into place, clean and perfectly tousled. His skin gleamed as if he'd just stepped out of a bath.

He snapped his fingers again, and suddenly he was wearing a deep cobalt blue tuxedo with icy blue leopard spots smattered diagonally across his chest.

"Now you do it." He helped me to my feet, and suddenly I was standing in front of a full-length, free-standing mirror. "If you were to bathe and style your hair and your clothes, what would the end result look like?"

I blinked at my reflection, a vision of self-indulgence topped with the most impressive bedhead I'd ever seen.

"Well, I'm supposed to be training, so I guess I'd put my hair up . . . " I began. Within seconds, my long blonde hair was clean and dry and gathered into a perfect high ponytail.

35

"Lovely," Chess hummed in approval. "What's next?"

Using the power of my imagination, I focused on my skin. A shower of magical sparkles washed over me, leaving my body clean and free from the evidence of last night's debauchery. My makeup came next: smoky eyes and blood-red lipstick . . . because if I was going to face Jack's wrath, I may as well look damn good doing it.

"You're making it difficult for me to restrain myself," Chess warned, and I realized he wasn't joking around. I could practically imagine him with flattened cat ears and a dramatic, swishing tail. Cats weren't shy about letting you know when they were seconds away from unleashing their brand of crazy. "You should probably put on some clothes before I forget my manners."

Laughing under my breath, I imagined my favorite outfit that I wore to spin class on chilly Saturdays—a black leotard with mesh panels that ran down my legs and straps that crisscrossed down my shoulders and across my bare back. I added a pair of white sneakers and an ultra-cropped hot pink sweatshirt that showed off just a hint of cleavage.

I spun around to face Chess, who was eyeing me with pure lust.

"If you're trying to leave this room unfucked, that outfit is . . . not helpful."

I smirked and shrugged at him. "It's comfy as hell. It's designed to give me full range of motion."

"Yes . . . I can tell . . . " he purred while sidling up

to me. His hand slipped around my waist, then caressed my ass before sliding between my legs. He let out a low, irritated growl. "There's only one flaw in the design. How am I supposed to fuck you through this contraption?"

"You're not—that's the point," I snickered while pushing him away. I walked over to the nightstand and grabbed Ransom's gold ring, slipping it onto my thumb. "If you're a good kitty, maybe I'll let you tear this thing off of me tonight."

Chess's grin spread from ear to ear, and his brilliant green eyes sparkled like emeralds. Then he gave me an obedient nod and went to open the door.

"Of course I'll be good. I'll be anything you want me to be."

I had to do a double take, but Chess simply stood by the door, patiently waiting for me to join him.

The shift in his demeanor was so drastic, so obvious, that I glanced down at the gold band around my thumb. Even though I'd been told that the Ring of Temptation could make others bend to the will of whoever wore it, I hadn't expected it to be so strong, or to work on demons.

I'd just put it on, and I could immediately feel the temptation to keep it and use it to my advantage.

But the Ring of Temptation didn't belong to me. For all I knew, the Red Queen might've infused it with evil magic, or put some kind of tracking spell on it. Even though I was already running late for my training session with Jack, I had to find Ransom first.

The sooner he got his ring back, the better.

As I walked through the halls of the castle, the scent of fresh flowers and spiced breakfast foods filled my nostrils, mixing with the lingering odor of burning candles and incense. I hurried past sculptures of strange animals and gargoyles, all made of frosted crystal.

Their eyes seemed to follow me as they watched my every move, but even though it was creepy as fuck, I had more important things on my mind.

I gently knocked on Ransom's door and waited for a response. When there was none, I slowly turned the knob and peeked inside.

He was lying in a luxurious hospital bed, propped up with a complicated arrangement of pillows that prevented him from putting too much weight on his outstretched wings. Strange cages were wrapped around the thick bandages, keeping his wings from bending or shifting. The black feathered tips were the only part of them that were visible outside of the bandages, which were still oozing blackish-green poison.

White sheets were tucked around Ransom's waist, and one side of his handsome face was nestled against yet another pillow. One of his demon horns was buried deep between two pillows while the other one curled in a skyward spiral. He looked so vulnerable in that moment.

I slipped into the room and let the door click shut behind me. Ransom immediately snapped awake, his body tense, his eyes wild, until he registered who I was.

"Alice," he croaked, his voice dry and scratchy and barely audible.

"I came by to check on you, my king."

Ransom's gaze softened and he relaxed against his pillows as I stepped to his bedside.

He looked up at me with half-lidded eyes, his face pale and beaded with sweat. The pain in his expression made my stomach twist. I lifted a leg and sat on the edge of the bed, our thighs brushing against each other through the sheets.

"How are you feeling?" I asked, reaching out to gingerly stroke his cheek.

"Like I've been trampled by a herd of grumple-hoofs." He tried to smirk but failed. Although I didn't have the first clue what a grumplehoof was, I raised an eyebrow in concern. Now was not the time to be brave.

"Is the White Queen giving you anything for the pain?"

A weak sneer passed across his face as he faintly shook his head.

"Apparently it's better to feel the pain with this type of poison. As soon as it's drawn out of my body, the pain will be gone."

I sucked in a breath through my teeth.

"It seems pretty bad."

"I can handle it. Especially if you keep wearing

39

outfits like that one. I'm getting stronger by the second," he sighed, although his tired eyes betrayed him.

Afraid that my touch might cause him more pain than comfort, I let my fingers fall away from his cheek and return to my lap. I bit my lip, feeling my heart sink in my chest.

But Ransom just grinned.

"Don't bite your lip, bunny. That's *my* job."

"I'm sorry, my king."

I couldn't help smiling, although it didn't last long. I cleared my throat and looked up at him.

"No, really . . . I'm sorry about putting you in this position. If I'd actually cut off the Red Queen's head, none of this would've happened."

Ransom studied me with heavy-lidded eyes.

"I disagree. For all you know, we might've been killed before we ever made it upstairs. Don't worry, pet. We'll come up with another plan. A better plan. The White Knight is good at that sort of thing. How was your first lesson with him?"

My eyes drifted up to the ceiling.

"Uhhh . . . actually . . . I haven't had it yet. I overslept."

Ransom's eye twitched in disapproval.

"He won't be happy about that. He isn't used to having his orders disobeyed. If you want to get on his good side, take my advice and go find him before he finds you."

"I will, but I had to give you this first." I slid the

gold ring off my thumb and pressed it into Ransom's palm.

Within seconds, the glazed look in his eyes cleared and his posture straightened. He blinked at me in disbelief, confusion, and wonder etched across his handsome face.

"Alice . . . where did you . . . how did you manage to get this back from Roxanne?"

Crossing my legs, I shrugged and gave him a playful grin.

"It must've slipped off her finger when it was jammed up in my pussy."

He stared at the ring for a long moment before meeting my gaze again.

"Why, you clever, clever girl! You could've had so much power with magic like this, yet you choose not to keep it. I'm very proud of you, bunny."

Puffing my chest out in pride, I tossed my pony-tail over my shoulder.

"I don't know how to use it, and even if I did, I don't want that level of responsibility. My plate's already full enough as it is."

"All the more reason for you to find Jack and start your training," said Ransom. He twisted off the gold replica ring on his pinky and let it tumble to the floor. It bounced once, then shattered into a tiny cloud of glittering gold dust that evaporated into the air.

He held the true Ring of Temptation, examining it carefully before sliding it onto his pinky finger. It glowed brightly for a moment, then dimmed to a soft pulse. The second it stopped pulsing, Ransom's dark eyes began to glow in a warm shade of amber, almost like the magic had bonded to the cells in his body.

He took a deep breath, then let out a long, slow groan of satisfaction. It was the kind of sound that made my pussy clench . . . made my clit hum with anticipation.

Ransom's voice already sounded stronger.

Deeper.

And brimming with desire.

"You did well by returning my ring, bunny. I'm starting to feel better already. How would you like your reward?"

Something in his voice longed for me—I could hear it plain as day . . . clear as a bell. His eyes focused on my body, narrowing as they lingered over my curves. My leotard hadn't left much to the imagination, but if anyone in this castle had an imagination, it was Ransom.

"I'm sure you'll think of something," I teased with a flirtatious wink. "But not right now. You need your rest."

Ransom shot me a seductive grin that immediately made my panties melt.

"There are things I can do to you while resting in bed." He lifted his arm and curled a finger once, then twice, motioning for me to come closer. "Why don't you sit on your king's lap so I can give you a kiss?"

Even without the bunny mask or my collar, I obediently lowered my eyes and nodded.

"Yes, my king."

I crawled into his lap, spreading my legs wide as I

straddled him over the sheets. He pulled my hips hard against his, and I held back a whimper, unable to ignore the pain coming from the bruises on my inner thighs. After hours and hours of Chess's relentless pounding, my body still needed time to recover.

Fat chance of that happening.

Resting my hands on Ransom's bare chest, I closed my eyes and leaned in to kiss him softly on the lips. His taste was just like I remembered—firm and warm and tempting. I couldn't resist indulging in another sensual kiss when he squeezed my ass and groaned in pleasure.

His fingers traced along my neck, my collarbone, then ran along my ribs and waist. Then he lifted me with his strong hands, repositioned his dick, then pulled me down to sit on top of his robust erection.

Ransom's eyes roamed over my body, hot and possessive. His arms went to work, guiding my hips to rub up and down the length of his cock. Heat bloomed between his exposed hard flesh and the thin fabric of my leotard, making my clit come alive from the friction.

"Yes . . . " he groaned under his breath. "Just like that, Alice. You're making me stronger."

"How?" I shuddered as I kept humping him.

"Incubus demons feed on sexual energy . . . " he murmured. His biceps continued to flex and curl as he held tight onto me. "I don't have to fuck you. I don't have to come. I don't have to make *you* come, either . . . even though I'd certainly like to. Although . . . it's better if I don't give you what you

43

want. I'd rather feed on this energy for as long as possible."

My eyes flashed wide in surprise.

"Is *that* the reason why you were obsessed with edging me for hours and hours back when we were at your casino? Because it makes you stronger?"

He let out a wicked laugh, and in that moment, it was the most beautiful sound I'd ever heard him make.

"You'll have to wear this outfit again once I'm fully recovered," he breathed into my ear. "You don't know how hard it is for me to not tear a hole in the crotch and fuck your greedy little cunt."

"You could do it," I panted while grinding harder against him. "You could tear it to shreds. I'll just imagine a new leotard after we're done."

Ransom shook his head and eased up on the pressure.

"No . . . I'd rather watch my slutty little bunny squirm on my cock. You're getting close, aren't you?"

"Yeah."

Ransom's gaze darkened with desire and hunger. He took my chin in his hand and shot me a warning look.

"Answer me properly, pet."

"Yes, my king. I'm getting close!"

"Good girl."

His fingers stroked up my inner thighs and cupped my steaming hot center. I gasped at the sensation of his nails scratching against my clit through the wet fabric of my leotard and my soaking panties. Ransom's touch was feather-light at first, teasing and tantalizing, but it wasn't enough.

I needed more.

"Please," I whimpered as I thrust myself against his hand. "Please, my king. Let me come!"

Ransom chuckled. "So eager. Don't worry, I'll give you what you need. But not right now."

He pulled his hand away and grinned in satisfaction.

"You asshole!" I hissed. I shoved a hand down and started rubbing, trying my hardest to get myself off.

The King of Clubs wasn't having any of it.

He grabbed my wrist and clamped it down against my outer thigh.

"You're such a good girl, Alice. Look at the wet spot you're making on your clothes."

I wriggled and rocked against his hard cock, so fucking desperate to come that I wanted to cry. I shuddered and gripped the bedsheets with my free hand until my knuckles turned white.

"Give me your panties, and I'll make you come."

I blinked in confusion at him.

"You'll need to let go of my hand so I can take off my clothes."

Ransom shook his head.

"You're not wearing your collar, bunny. Use your imagination. Take off your soaking wet panties and put them in my hand."

Woozy with lust, I nodded my head and did as I was told. A hot pink cheeky bikini trimmed in lace suddenly materialized in my left hand. I gave it to Ransom, who held it up for inspection. He brought it to his nose and inhaled deeply, then sighed in approval. The entire crotch panel was soaked and glistening with my juices.

"Good girl. You can start riding me again."

A wave of relief washed over me as I began thrusting my hips against him, using his hard body for my enjoyment. My clit was getting even more stimulation without the panties in the way, but it didn't last long. I was too distracted at the sight of Ransom conjuring a teapot on the small bedside table.

I watched in confusion, then complete and utter shock as he lifted the lid, dropped my panties into the steaming hot water, and set the lid gently back into place.

"What the fuck are you doing?" I gasped.

"Making tea, obviously," he replied as he conjured a matching teacup. "It's purely for medicinal purposes."

My jaw fell as I shot him a dubious look.

"Medicinal purposes? Are you fucking kidding me?"

"Not at all," Ransom replied with a deviant grin. "It'll help me recover faster while you're having your lesson with Jack."

I didn't know whether to be flattered, horrified, or humiliated, but I felt some degree of all of those things.

"You don't need to make pussy tea out of my

underwear!" I snapped at him. "Just fucking *fuck* me already! Jack can fucking *wait*!"

Ransom shot me a skeptical look. "Oh . . . I don't think he can. I think Jack's done waiting for you."

The second Ransom's eyes flicked beyond my shoulder and remained there, my blood went cold. My desperate, eager humping ground to a halt and I gritted my teeth.

"Jack's standing behind me, isn't he?"

"Yes." Ransom gave me a smug, seductive grin. "And I don't think he's here to play with us. You'd better hop along, bunny."

I scowled at Ransom, wishing with all my heart that this was just another one of his twisted games. Summoning all the powers of my imagination, I envisioned a scenario where I'd turn around and discover he and I were all alone in his room, with no sign of Jack.

I took a deep breath, then turned to look over my shoulder.

Fuck.

Jack was definitely there.

Suited up to his neck in full armor, the White Knight looked anything but chivalrous.

CHAPTER

FOUR

ALICE

I turned around and locked eyes with Jack. He was standing in the doorway, his arms crossed and his jaw set. His red eyes glowered at me, making it clear he was more than just a little pissed off. He didn't need to say a word—his expression said enough. I didn't need to know how angry he was, either.

It was palpable.

Cold anger radiated off of him like the icy winds of a polar vortex.

I couldn't believe my luck.

I should've known he'd show up at the worst possible moment. Yet, he tried to maintain some composure.

"You're late."

Ignoring Ransom's bemused expression and Jack's unwavering stare, I scrambled off the demon's lap with what little remaining dignity I still had.

It wasn't much.

I'd lost my panties and had a huge wet spot in the

crotch of my leotard, which now felt like it was giving me an impressive camel toe.

My face flushed red with embarrassment, but this sort of thing was well within my wheelhouse. My parents were celebrities. I'd grown up on a reality TV show. I liked to party and I liked to fuck. I'd been caught by the paparazzi in so many compromising situations that I knew how to play this sort of thing to my advantage.

Smoothing my ponytail, I playfully twirled the end of it around my finger and brought my shoulders back, making my tits stand out. Then I gave Jack one of my most authentic pouts.

"I overslept. Sorry."

His scathing gaze slid down at me, glaring with disdain.

"You're not sorry. But you *will* be."

The iciness of his tone sent a chill through my bones, and I immediately stopped twirling my hair. My stomach turned as I wondered exactly how much trouble I was in.

I glanced back one last time at Ransom, whose smug expression remained unchanged. If anyone could get me out of this mess, it was a demon with an all-access pass to Hell and an obsession with my pussy.

But no . . .

All that fucker did was lift his teacup to toast me!

My jaw fell open again as he took a hefty gulp of tea. Before I could respond, Jack had already whisked me out of the room and shut the door.

I was fuming.

Absolutely fuming.

I was such a dumbass—I should've held onto that Ring of Temptation a bit longer. I could've used it against both of these guys.

Jack's voice sliced through the tense silence like a scalpel.

"How dare you make me hunt you down like an animal."

I shot him a defiant look.

"You're a vampire. I thought you'd be into that sort of thing."

I swear he growled before he stormed down the hall in long, quick strides. His cloak swirled behind his wake, leaving me to practically run to catch up with him. I hated how small and insignificant he made me feel.

"Look, I'm sorry I overslept, but dawn is way too early to train," I reasoned as I followed Jack down the hallway of the White Queen's crystal castle. "I haven't even had time to grab a coffee."

"Perhaps you would've been on time if you hadn't stayed up all night with Chess," he replied coldly. "From dawn to dusk, you belong to me."

"What about breakfast? When am I supposed to eat?"

"That's not my concern. Training you how to use the Vorpal Sword is my only concern."

"I'll learn faster if I'm not starving," I pointed out. I knew we were getting close to the Great Hall, because I could smell the tantalizing scents of fresh food. They were making my mouth water.

"You're not starving," Jack scoffed. "You've never known true hunger."

"Yes I have!" I argued, and stopped walking. Jack whirled around and I pointed at my stomach. "Listen!"

Right on cue, my stomach let out a ferocious growl.

Jack's mouth twisted from a restrained scowl to a cunning grin.

"Very well. You *should* eat to your heart's content. Who am I to deny you?"

To my pleasant surprise, Jack returned to my side and escorted me into the Great Hall.

I thought I'd died and gone to brunch heaven.

The air was perfumed with the irresistible aromas of a decadent feast. The Great Hall was bathed in soft blue light, streaming through large frosted windows, giving a surreal glow to the opulent setting. Long, elegantly draped tables stretched across the room, adorned with fine linens and sparkling silverware, inviting me to indulge in the culinary delights.

At one end of the hall, a magnificent buffet table was piled with a cornucopia of freshly baked bread, croissants, and pastries. Towering platters held stacks of fluffy, golden pancakes and waffles, drizzled with rich maple syrup and topped with fresh berries and dollops of whipped cream.

Nearby, a pair of chefs expertly flipped omelets,

all made to order with a selection of cheeses, herbs, and fresh vegetables. Another chef stood behind a table, carving thick slices of succulent, honey-glazed ham and tender roast beef.

Rows of chafing dishes were sending out faint wisps of steam, revealing scrambled eggs that looked as soft as clouds. I saw piles of crispy bacon, savory sausages, and seasoned potatoes.

Their tantalizing scent mingled with the rich aroma of freshly brewed coffee and an assortment of teas. Alongside, an array of fresh juice—orange, cranberry, apple, and more—all of them glistening like precious gems in elegant pitchers.

The clinking of cutlery and the hum of excited conversations filled the air, punctuated by soft background music. People from the White Queen's court mingled and moved around. Some of them sat at tables scattered around the hall, while others were drifting from one table of food to another.

My eyes lit up with excitement and I made a beeline for the juice table.

"Mimosas? Oh *hell* yeah!"

I grabbed a champagne glass, then found a plate and started loading it up. Normally I'd have some self-restraint when going out to brunch, but I'd never seen anything like this decadent display before.

Restraint had no business being in a place like this.

And also, I hadn't had breakfast. Or dinner the night before. Come to think of it, I couldn't remember the last time I'd eaten.

So yeah. I was fucking starving.

Jack followed behind me in silence as I found a table and sat down. He politely shook his head when I offered him a tender biscuit.

"What about an apricot tart?"

"No."

I popped the mini tart into my mouth, then finished my mimosa. To my sheer wonder, the glass instantly refilled itself. I gulped half of it before digging into my scrambled eggs.

"You want a waffle?"

"No."

"Bacon?"

"No."

"You don't want anything at all?"

Shooting me a curious side-eye, Jack sat back in his chair, then held back a smile. Good. He was finally warming up to my charms.

"All I want is to train you, Alice. Surely you must be getting full."

I glanced down at my plate. I wasn't just full—I was *stuffed*—but everything was so damn delicious. I studied the remaining syrupy waffle sitting all alone in a small pool of butter. I didn't need it . . .

But I *wanted* it.

I polished off my second mimosa and washed down that incredible waffle with a third drink. By the time I'd finished, I was feeling grateful for wearing a spandex leotard.

"*Now* I'm full," I told Jack as I pushed my chair back and stood up. My head spun so hard that I

leaned forward and grabbed the edge of the table. It
had been a while since I'd done any day drinking, and
all those mimosas had gone straight to my head.

"Come along," said Jack, curling a gloved hand
around my arm. "We have work to do."

He led me through the palace of white stone
and sparkling ice, navigating the frosty grounds
until we reached a large private courtyard. It was
surrounded by tall, imposing walls of crystalline
ice that seemed to shimmer in the pale blue
light. Frosted windows diffused the sunlight, I
assumed to keep Jack safe from the powerful
rays.

The cold, crisp air was a stark contrast to the
smoggy sunshine and heat of Los Angeles, and the
sultry darkness and warmth of the Rabbit Hole. My
breath formed small clouds as I exhaled.

The whimsical beauty of Wonderland was
breathtaking, but I was buzzed and my stomach was
more than full. I felt ready to burst. All I wanted at
that moment was to fall back into my soft bed and
sleep off my exhaustion.

"Here is where we will practice your swordsman-
ship," Jack explained, gesturing to the open space
before us. The ground was a mirror of smooth, slick
ice. It reflected the balcony that wrapped around the
entire space and the weapons mounted on the icy
walls below.

I could name some of them . . . sword, crossbow,
dagger, spear. But there were more than I'd ever
dreamed of, all hanging from the balcony

surrounding me. I wondered if I'd be obligated to master them all . . .

Metal ball with spikes. Thor's hammer. Pokey-pointy-stabby thinger. It seemed like the only weapon missing from the wall was the Vorpal Sword. It hung at Jack's side, the hilt caressing his narrow hips with a dangerous, yet sensual allure.

I took a step onto the smooth floor and immediately slipped and fell on my ass.

"What the hell?" I groaned as I carefully pulled myself back onto my feet. "Exactly why are we practicing in an ice skating rink?"

Jack was wearing another one of his faint, yet sinister grins.

"Training on ice demands exceptional balance and footwork. You're not merely going to learn the art of the blade—you're going to learn the dance of agility and precision."

I jutted out my chin in defiance.

"What if I don't want *you* for a dance partner?"

"Oh, Alice . . . you and I are not going to dance," he murmured. "You're going to *run*. You kept me waiting five hours this morning, so that's how long you will run. Begin."

He shooed me away with a bored motion of his hand.

Well . . .

He tried.

"Five hours? Are you serious?" I protested, clutching my stomach as it churned from the mimosas and all-you-can-eat brunch buffet. "I can't *run* right now!"

"Perhaps you need some motivation," Jack smirked, his red eyes flashing with cruel intentions. He whispered something under his breath, and suddenly a bone-chilling howl split the air.

I whipped around to see a pack of terrifying black monster-dogs gathering in one corner of the court-yard. Their eyes glowed bright orangey-red, like fire. One of them howled again, revealing long, razor sharp fangs.

"What the hell are those?" I trembled as my stomach turned.

"Abyssal hounds," Jack replied with a twisted grin. "They prefer to disembowel their prey and eat it while it's still alive." To my shock and horror, instead of protecting me, the White Knight leaped twelve feet into the air and landed on the balcony above me. He pulled up a chair and sat down as if he had box seats to a Broadway show. "They look hungry. You'd better start running."

The abyssal hounds were fanning out, growling, and stalking towards me. I let out a shriek of terror and took off in the opposite direction, scrambling and slipping on the ice.

I forgot all about Jack as the monsters gained on me. I don't remember how long I screamed. I did everything I could to get away from their snarling, snapping jaws.

I pushed my aching body to its limits, regretting

the mimosas and that extra waffle. And the potatoes. And the ham. And the eggs.

Uggggh . . . the eggs.

Everything in my stomach was sloshing around, and suddenly I couldn't scream anymore. I was too busy puking all over the ice . . . all over myself, until I slipped and fell and got up and ran and did it all over again.

The hounds charged at me relentlessly, never giving me a break. When I dared to slow down, one of them bit the side of my knee, tearing a hole in the mesh of my leotard. My legs felt like they were on fire, but the terror of being eaten alive kept me going.

A powerful cramp seized my left calf, then another one took hold of my right. I collapsed in a pitiful wet heap on the ice. Glowing red eyes and vicious snarls surrounded me as I wailed and cried and panted, covered in vomit and sweat.

If this was how I was going to die, at least it would be over soon. I curled into a ball and threw back my head to expose my neck. I didn't want to be disemboweled. I wanted them to go straight for the jugular.

Make it quick.

Please . . . just make it stop!

I closed my eyes and sucked in what I hoped would be my final breath.

Without warning, the hounds vanished as quickly as they'd appeared. I rolled onto my back, gasping for air, and found Jack standing over me.

"Giving up so soon?"

I lay there catching my breath, waiting for him to offer me a hand and help me up. When it was clear that wasn't going to happen, I stumbled to my feet.

"What do you . . . what do you mean?" I forced out between deep breaths. My voice was hoarse and raw from screaming at the top of my lungs. "I was running for . . . for at least . . . a couple hours!"

Jack shook his head in disappointment.

"You ran for exactly seven minutes. You still have two-hundred and ninety-three remaining. Perhaps you need something more motivating than abyssal hounds. Shall I conjure a bandersnatch to chase you?"

My eyes widened in both horror and rage.

"Are you telling me that you did that on *purpose*?" I seethed. My voice was broken and raw. "You psycho shitbag motherfucker! You tried to *kill* me!"

I raised my hand to slap him.

"Don't do it," he warned.

I did it.

Channeling all of my fury and pain, I let my hand fucking *fly* across his beautiful face.

I instantly regretted it.

White hot agony spread through my palm and every finger on my hand. I was sure every bone was broken. I expected my hand to slap the shit out of the soft skin covering Jack's cheek—not bang it full-force into a fucking block of ice.

Jack flinched in slow motion, as if merely annoyed, before shoving his weight against me and curling his hand around my throat. His fingers were cold and firm, but they didn't choke the life out of me. He held me close, staring deep into my eyes with the expression of a shark about to attack.

"If I was going to kill you, I'd do it in a way that made you enjoy every second of your demise," he said coolly. From this close, I could smell the scent of his leather armor, and the hint of balsam fir coming from his hair, like he'd spent the night hiking through a forest of pine trees.

His cool thumb stroked along my warm, sweaty throat, pressing against the throbbing artery in my neck. The sound of my racing heartbeat filled my ears, and something shifted in Jack's gaze, making me wonder if he heard it, too.

His eyes clouded with longing, and his lips parted, revealing sharp, white incisors. He drew in a shaky breath before letting out a soft, wistful sigh.

"In my eyes, you are nothing but a lazy little lump of spoiled meat rotting in my hand. However, in the eyes of my queen, you are Wonderland's last hope."

He abruptly let go of my neck, and I stumbled backward, slipping on the ice before crumpling into a heap while cradling my aching hand. Tears stung my eyes as I realized this guy didn't give two shits about how famous I was back home, who my parents were, or how much money or influence or connections my family had.

"If I'm so important, then why are you being so awful to me?"

An amused smile passed briefly across his lips.
It faded fast.

"I never said you were important. You're more of a last resort. Your actions do not only affect you," he lectured. "They affect the suffering people of Wonderland. Every minute that you spend indulging in sleeping and fucking and eating and drinking to excess is another minute that the people of Wonderland suffer and die at the hands of the Red Queen. The only way to save them from her tyranny is for you to master the Vorpal Sword as soon as possible."

The harsh reality of his words cut me to the core, and I felt more aware and ashamed of my selfish behavior than I'd ever thought capable. People were suffering and dying, and I had the power to stop it.

And I wasn't.

Because of what? An all-night fuckfest with the Cheshire Cat? Free refills on mimosas?

Flashbacks came flooding into my mind; me finding out my boyfriend was cheating when his side chick's money shot video went viral . . .

Me finding out secondhand that little kids in sweatshops were building my shoe empire . . .

Me getting booed off stage at a charity gala for those same exploited children . . .

Me sitting in a bathroom toilet stall as my entire world crumbled all around me . . .

But at least I was still alive.

It was more than I could say for some of the people here in Wonderland. People like Callister's brother.

Tears stung at my eyes but I immediately wiped them away. It wasn't going to do any good to beat myself up . . . not when Jack was already kicking my ass. I silently vowed to show him just how wrong he was about me.

Maybe I didn't know how to defeat the Red Queen . . .

But I could learn.

"Fine, I'll try harder," I said from the ground. "But you don't have to be so mean to me."

Jack's nimble fingers unfastened the buckles of his armor, then let it slide to the frozen floor. I watched him roll up the sleeves of his shirt, unable to look away from the ropes of veins that highlighted his muscular forearms.

"Oh, Alice . . . you haven't even *begun* to see the depths of how cruel I can be. By all means . . . test me if you like." He caught my gaze and lifted an eyebrow at me in warning. "But I don't recommend it."

I wasn't sure whether to obediently nod my head or shake it. In that moment, all I knew was that I had zero interest in testing the limits of the White Knight's cruelty.

"Now . . . you still owe me two-hundred and ninety-three minutes of running."

Somehow, I managed to drag myself back onto my feet. My hand was still throbbing in pain, but I was determined not to let him see it.

"I swear I'll make it up to you, especially if it doesn't have to be all at once. Please, Jack. Can we just get on with our lesson? I'll run some laps when we're done. I promise."

A flicker of crimson lit up his dark red eyes, giving me the smallest shred of hope.

"Very well," he conceded, his expression softening ever so slightly. "But remember, Alice, the stakes have never been higher. Wonderland is depending on you. I expect you to step up and become the warrior you were destined to be."

A warrior?

I almost scoffed at the thought.

It wasn't the first time I'd been told about my destiny to save Wonderland, but it was the first time I'd seriously pictured myself in that role.

"I'll try."

Jack shook his head, his long platinum hair catching on his shoulders. He seemed less imposing without all the bulky armor.

"No. You will not *try*. You are being personally trained by the Supreme Commander of the White Queen's army. You will *succeed*."

I swallowed hard as I fought against the light-headed sensation that had suddenly taken hold of me. He was the Supreme Commander of the White Queen's army? And I'd blown him off like he was some dinner theater wannabe version of an Arthurian knight of the Round Table?

Fuck.

No wonder he hated me.

Somehow, I needed to make it up to him.

"Alright. I won't try. I'll succeed. Where do we start?"

"I need to know what you know," he said simply. "Have you ever used a sword?"

Forgetting that I was covered in my own dried puke, I puffed up my chest with pride.

"For your information, I was on the fencing team back in middle school and junior high. I took second place in the state championship."

Again, Jack raised an eyebrow, this time skeptical. "Well, that's not nothing, but we're not dealing with foils here. This is real combat, with real blades, and real consequences."

"Trust me, I know what I'm doing," I insisted, trying to ignore the throbbing pain in my hand, in my legs, and throughout my entire body.

"We'll see soon enough."

Jack unsheathed the Vorpal Sword with a swift motion, the silver blade gleaming in the pale blue light of the private courtyard. The intricate engravings on its surface seemed to come alive as he held it, giving off an aura of power that made it look like a living, breathing thing.

"Here." He pulled a heavy, cumbersome practice sword off the wall and handed it to me. "You'll start with this. It'll help you get used to the weight and feel of a real weapon."

I took the sword awkwardly into my numb fingers, wincing at the unexpected strain it put on my muscles. It was a far cry from the finesse of a delicate fencing foil.

This thing weighed a ton, dragging my arm down with each attempt to lift it. I couldn't help but feel a pang of resentment towards Jack for giving me such a heavy weapon when the elegant Vorpal Sword looked light as a feather.

"Come at me," Jack ordered, taking a defensive stance. "Let's see what your years of fencing have taught you."

I motioned to his armor that was now lying on the ground.

"Shouldn't you put your armor back on?"

Jack shot me a bored expression.

"Why? You won't make contact with me."

Arrogant prick.

Didn't he hear me say that I won second place at my fencing team's finals?

Gritting my teeth, I lunged at Jack with all my strength, trying to strike him with the tip of my practice sword. My movements were slow and clumsy compared to the gracefulness of his own. He easily sidestepped my attack, clearly unimpressed by what he saw.

"You are painfully predictable, Alice." He circled around me like he was part abyssal hound. "You need to learn how to adapt and think on your feet. Fencing has taught you basic movements, but you lack imagination."

I growled and made another attempt to land a hit, only to be met with a yawn as Jack effortlessly dodged my strike once again.

"Your form is sloppy. And your footwork is a

mess," he observed while dodging my attacks with ease. The icy air bit at my exposed skin as I lunged, parried, and dodged under Jack's watchful eye. My cheeks flushed with a mixture of anger and embarrassment as he continued to criticize my technique and my abilities.

I silently cursed him, unable to ignore the smell of my own vomit or the soreness that radiated through my body after running from abyssal hounds. My long night with Chess only made my body hurt worse. My muscles screamed in protest, but I stubbornly pushed myself harder, refusing to give in to exhaustion.

But as we continued practicing, I couldn't help feeling more and more disheartened. Every swing of the practice sword felt slow and clumsy in comparison to Jack's effortless movements. The more I struggled, the more I realized just how far I had to go.

I clenched my fists, fighting the urge to scream at him, to cry, to give up.

That was exactly what he expected from me.

I refused to give him that satisfaction.

Instead, I channeled all of my frustration into proving Jack wrong, diving back into his exercises with renewed determination. My leotard and cropped sweatshirt were soaked with sweat. My body trembled with exhaustion, but I refused to back down.

"Enough," Jack abruptly commanded. "You're done for today."

I blinked in confusion. Was he giving me a water

break? I looked around the room in a daze. Through the frost-covered windows, an eerie twilight glow had pushed its way in and taken over the icy courtyard.

"Should I run laps?"

Jack shook his head and sheathed his sword.

"Not now. Tomorrow."

Collapsing to my knees on the frozen floor, I fought back the tears that threatened to spill over as I realized just how utterly drained I was—both physically, and mentally.

"Get up," Jack ordered, his voice devoid of any warmth or sympathy as he stared down at me with those piercing crimson eyes. "You still have a long way to go, Alice, but you've made progress today."

Wait—what?

I'd made progress?

Did he just give me a compliment?

Drawing on the last dregs of my strength, I forced myself to stand, my legs quivering like jelly beneath me as I struggled to maintain my composure.

"We'll meet here tomorrow." He paused to catch my gaze, shooting me a look of warning. "At dawn."

"Okay," I nodded, trying to catch my breath. My voice was hoarse from exhaustion and unshed tears. "I swear I'll be here on time."

"See that you are," Jack replied. Then, in one swift movement, he gathered his armor and disappeared into the shadows, letting the darkness swallow him whole.

JEKKA WILDE

CHAPTER
FIVE
ALICE

I wanted to die.

That's how much my body hurt.

I'd paid a shit-ton of money to booty boot camp trainers, although none of them had pushed me half this hard.

And the White Knight was doing it for free.

He'd terrorized me with demon dogs, made me run til I puked, kicked my ass with the Vorpal Sword, and expected me to be ready to go bright and early again at dawn.

Fucking sadist.

My burning limbs were heavy . . . so heavy. Even my neck was sore. How could holding up my head be this much work? A hot shower had done Jack shit to soothe my screaming muscles.

Speaking of Jack, I wanted to hate him . . .

But I was too tired.

I'd never known exhaustion like this . . . the

feeling of being so sore, so tired, so completely empty. My mind could only perform basic tasks that I could do without thinking.

Take a piss.

Brush my teeth.

Turn on the shower.

Wash my body and my hair.

I didn't bother with makeup or doing anything with my hair besides run a comb through it. I wasn't even able to conjure a plate of food. I was lucky I'd found a cup so I could drink some water.

I dressed in warm, comfy clothes—an oversized sweater with leggings and Uggs—then forced one foot in front of the other until I was standing at the entrance of the Great Hall.

The air was filled with the soft murmur of voices and the clinking of cutlery against plates. I stepped through the doors, bare-faced, with wet hair, realizing how underdressed I was.

And I was too tired to give a single fuck.

Instead, I let the warmth of the room envelop me like a soft blanket as I wandered inside. Chandeliers cast flickering golden light across the polished wood tables and fine china plates, their reflections dancing on the walls.

Callister, Hatter, and Chess were already sitting at one of the long tables, deep in conversation. From the looks of it, they'd already been drinking for a while. Callister lounged in an overstuffed chair beside them, puffing on a hookah that released deep purple smoke.

The smell of roasted meats, vegetables, and stewed fruits hung thick in the air, and my stomach growled at the tantalizing smells, reminding me of my ill-fated, overindulgent brunch.

I wouldn't be making *that* mistake again.

Hatter's eyes met mine and he tipped his hat in my honor, revealing his wily grin. "Ah, Alice, there you are. Join us, won't you?"

I gave him a weak smile as I came over and pulled out a chair, sinking into it with a groan.

"You look dead on your feet, darling," Chess purred, swirling the remains of the wine in his glass. His Cheshire grin widened. "Did the big, bad White Knight wear you out already?"

"I'm worse than worn out, in case you haven't noticed."

Callister chuckled darkly, his eyes glinting in the candlelight. "Oh, come now," he smirked, "it can't have been that bad. Don't tell me he's broken you on your first day."

"I'm not broken," I argued, although I wasn't completely sure. "I just didn't think he'd spend all day torturing me."

Callister's eyes lit up the second I said the word 'torture.'

"You didn't think learning to fight would be easy, did you?"

I shook my head, then groaned at how sore my neck was.

"I was expecting something more . . . more . . . " I trailed off, trying to think of the right words. "I was

71

expecting my lessons to be more formal. But Jack's method seems to be throwing me in the deep end to see if I can swim. The guy's a sadist."

Callister snickered while purple smoke curled from the corners of his grin. "Jack does tend to play rough."

I grimaced, rubbing the latest bruise to appear on my arm. I had so many that I'd lost count.

"You forgot to fix yourself a plate, dear. Would you like me to escort you to the tables?" Chess murmured while motioning to the long buffet lines at the other end of the room. They were the same tables from brunch, but now they seemed so far away.

My shoulders fell at the thought of having to stand up and move my body.

"That's sweet of you, but I'm gonna need a minute. I might be stuck in this chair for a while."

Hatter's mismatched eyes twinkled beneath the brim of his tattered top hat. "Fret not, fair Alice. A growing warrior needs proper sustenance." He waved his hand across an empty space on the table, then slid a plate of tarts and cupcakes toward me. "Sugar will give you strength."

I smiled weakly and pushed the plate away. "Sugar will give me zits." The cupcakes looked incredible, but I already knew I'd regret eating a bunch of junk food. Now was not the time to indulge.

It was time to nourish and fuel my body with vitamins and nutrients.

Especially if I was going to get my ass handed to me all over again at the ass-crack of dawn.

"I was thinking of something more like roast veggies, grilled chicken, and some brown rice. Can you make that happen?"

"With pleasure," said Chess. Within seconds a plate materialized in front of me, complete with silverware and a napkin. I would've thrown my arms around him if they weren't so tired.

As I dug into my dinner, my wicked boys continued their mindless drunken chatter, bickering about the meaning behind Chess's grin.

"He always acts like he knows something we don't," Hatter complained. Callister just rolled his eyes.

"He's a cat. He's probably grinning at his reflection. Everyone knows cats are insufferable in their vanity."

Chess grinned even wider. "Perhaps I smile to keep you from guessing what I'm truly thinking."

Hatter furrowed his brows in curiosity. "So, the grin is a riddle? I love riddles! Here's one—I speak without a mouth and I hear without ears. I have no body, but I come alive with the wind. What am I?"

Callister let out a rare lighthearted laugh.

"Pffft, you come alive if someone brushes up against you in a crowded room!"

As the three of them tried to solve the riddle, my attention zeroed in on the plate in front of me. My fork scraped against the porcelain as I shoveled food into my mouth, each bite a blur of desperate sustenance. The savory aroma of my dinner filled my nostrils, and each bite brought a satisfying warmth to my stomach.

My muscles relaxed just a little bit more with every mouthful, losing their sharp, painful edge. I felt a warmth spreading through my limbs, healing me so well that I was tempted to pour a glass of wine and try to solve Hatter's riddle.

But no . . .

I needed to make better choices.

Staying up late and drinking and solving riddles would only make tomorrow's practice session with Jack a million times worse. I didn't know how . . . but I didn't doubt he'd find a way to do it.

Since I'd skipped the wine, I grabbed two cupcakes and pushed my chair away from the table.

"Thanks for dinner, Chess. I'm going to go check on Ransom and see how he's doing. I'll see you guys around."

"Let us know if you need a bedtime story," Chess replied.

"Or a lullaby," added Hatter.

"Or if you just want to fuck," Callister said.

He wasn't one to mince words.

"I'll let you know," I told them, then left the Great Hall.

I walked down the brightly lit corridors of the icy castle, wondering how the torches didn't melt the frost that glittered all over the walls.

Then I remembered that this was Wonderland— things worked differently here.

As I came around the corner, I saw Amari stepping out of Ransom's room before closing the door behind her.

"Is Ransom alright?" I asked with concern. I lifted up the cupcakes I'd brought. "I thought he'd like a snack."

She gave me a soft, warm smile.

"He's sleeping now, but his health is greatly improved. All the poison has finally been drawn from his wings."

My eyes lit up with relief and excitement.

"That's great news!"

Amari nodded with enough enthusiasm that her long purple coils bounced with a life all their own.

"It truly is. He should be able to leave the infirmary in a day or two," she replied with a reassuring smile. "But I wouldn't wake him now. The more sleep he gets, the faster he'll heal."

My gaze wandered down to the two cupcakes in my hands. Then I held them out to Amari.

"Want one?"

"Thank you," she said, taking the shimmering pink and yellow frosted one. "Moonblush berry is my favorite."

"I have no idea what flavors I grabbed. I just thought they were pretty."

Amari nodded, then motioned to the pearlescent rainbow-frosted one I was still holding. "That flavor's dreamdew drop. It tastes like . . . well, like a dreamdew drop."

Unsure if she meant dreamdew drops tasted like ass or like champagne, I watched as she started to delicately peel the silver foil wrapper off the side of her cupcake.

"Would you like to join me for a walk in the ice gardens? Unless you have other plans, of course."

"Oh, I don't have any plans besides going to bed early." I hesitated for a moment, caught in disbelief at the words that had just come out of my mouth. I, Alice Darling, who always knew where the hottest parties in Malibu were, was going to bed *early*?

On purpose?

When the fuck had I become such an adult?

"My new personal trainer wants to meet at dawn," I added.

With an elegant wave of her hand, Amari motioned for me to walk with her.

"Yes, that sounds like something Jacques would require of you. I know he can be quite demanding. That's what makes him the most qualified candidate for the task."

I considered asking her to define the word 'demanding,' because it didn't sound like we had the same interpretation. But I was distracted by something else she'd said.

"Amari, can I ask why you call Jack 'Jacques'? Am I saying his name wrong?"

She gave a little hum, like she was reminiscing about something that had happened a long, long time ago.

"No . . . he'll answer to either. I call him Jacques because that's his name. His given name. He wasn't born in Wonderland like the rest of us. He came from Earth, just like you."

I almost dropped my cupcake.

"Really? How?"

"The same way you did. He followed Winston through a rabbit hole."

"Winston?" I racked my brain trying to remember where I'd heard that name before. "Ohhh! You mean the White Rabbit?"

With her mouth full of moonblush berry cupcake, all Amari could do was nod politely as we walked down yet another shimmering hallway. She finished chewing, then licked off the bit of frosting from her full bottom lip.

"The one and only. Winston's running an errand for me right now, but when he returns, he'll be so happy to see you. I can't tell you what a relief it is that you're finally here."

We stopped at a gleaming silver gate. I was surprised when Amari pushed it wide open and invited me inside. I thought there were special rules when it came to queens . . . like having butlers and footmen to do mundane tasks like opening gates.

As Amari and I stepped into the ice garden, I couldn't help but feel like I'd stepped into a winter wonderland. The crystalline structures and sculptures glittered in the soft, colorful light from above, casting an otherworldly glow on the frost-covered ground.

The ethereal vision spreading out in front of us

sparkled and shimmered under the dim, yet colorful colors of the deepest, darkest twilight. Soft, colorful lights moved around the garden, dancing over the ice, buzzing around the plants, creating a dazzling display.

The plants were a mix of greens, purples, and splashes of magenta, popping up everywhere despite the frosty sheen that covered them. Flowers were frozen in time, yet still moved enough to catch the light.

Amari motioned towards a bench that sat under a tree in the center of the garden. She walked so slowly that it seemed like she didn't care if we ever got to it. I think she just wanted to give me enough time to take everything in.

Turned out, I wanted every single second.

The snow crunched under my feet, echoing in the stillness. I marveled at the delicate icicles hanging from each branch from the tree beside the bench. I caught sight of the half-frozen waterfall before I heard the gentle trickle of water and the occasional chirping of birds that had made the garden their home.

I suddenly realized Amari was already sitting on the bench below the shimmering tree loaded with sparkling icicles. Taking in the crisp, fresh scent of winter berries and frost-covered trees, I stepped over the bench and sank down beside her.

"This place is incredible . . . " I let out a puff of warm breath, watching it disappear in front of my eyes. "How does anything grow here when it's so cold?"

"Easy. It adapts. Just like we do." Amari's presence exuded an air of serenity that put me at ease, despite the chaos that had recently become my life. Her eyes met mine, soft and welcoming. "I meant it when I said I'm grateful to finally have you here, Alice. Wonderland is suffering."

"I know." I hung my head, staring at the decadent cupcake in my hands. "It doesn't seem fair that I'm sitting here in a gorgeous garden, eating amazing food, and staying in a room that's nicer than most luxury hotels, when people are getting decapitated right and left."

Amari's expression became less dreamy and more pragmatic.

"Yes, well, it won't do us much good if our champion is malnourished and sleep-deprived."

"I get what you're saying, but here's the thing –" I swallowed hard, my voice wavering as I revealed my doubts. "Even with Jack's sword-fighting lessons, I don't know if I can defeat the Jabberwocky. Or the Red Queen. Like, I've never even been in a fight before, let alone one with magical monsters and psycho queens. What if I freeze up, or panic? What if I'm just not strong enough?"

Amari listened attentively, her expression never betraying judgment or disappointment. She seemed to understand my skepticism, which only made me appreciate her more.

"Your concerns are valid." She placed a warm hand on my shoulder. "You were brought to Wonderland for a reason, Alice. There is strength and power within you that even you don't fully comprehend yet."

Her words were meant to be reassuring, but they only intensified the knot of anxiety twisting in my gut.

The thought of fighting for my life, wielding the Vorpal Sword against nightmarish creatures and vengeful queens, sent shivers down my spine – and not from the cold. Could I really do this? Was there any chance that I, reality TV star from LA, could become the badass warrior Wonderland so desperately needed?

"How can you be so sure I can do this? You don't even know me."

"I know enough." Amari's lips curved into a mysterious smile. "You are the first Alice to arrive in Wonderland already grown. You have skills that the other Alices did not, and that will serve you well in the battle to come."

I frowned, recalling Callister's accusation that I was too old to be of any use. True, he'd found other uses for me, but being able to take the full length of his giant, freakish, insect cock wasn't going to save Wonderland.

"I thought being older wasn't exactly an advantage here. The other Alices were kids. They were a lot more imaginative than me."

"Nonsense." Amari gave my shoulder a gentle squeeze. I found her touch to be warm and comforting. "You underestimate yourself, Alice. While my previous Alices had youth and naiveté on their side, you have wisdom, instinct, and a strength of will that comes only with age and experience. You will prevail. I have no doubt."

Her unwavering faith in me was almost too much to handle. I didn't want to disappoint her, but the ugly truth was, I might fail. Wonderland might fall into darkness, and it would be all my fault.

Swallowing the lump in my throat, I looked directly at Amari. "You really think I can defeat the Jabberwocky?"

"Absolutely." Her eyes shone with such conviction that it was inspiring. "It's important to remember that you're not alone. You have allies here who will help prepare you for the challenges ahead."

"Even with your help, I still don't know why you chose me for this mission," I said before biting into my cupcake.

I was instantly grateful I'd only taken one.

I might've inhaled an entire plate of them otherwise.

The burst of dreamdew drop flavor was a brief distraction from my swirling thoughts. The berry's flavor exploded in my mouth, a vibrant fusion of sweet, tangy, and creamy notes that danced across my palate. As I chewed and swallowed, it released a blend of vanilla and exotic spices, giving a new meaning to the phrase 'comfort food.'

"I didn't choose you, Alice. Destiny did," Amari replied gently. "You possess a rare combination of strength, intelligence, and tenacity, which is precisely what Wonderland needs right now."

I snorted, feeling anything but strong or intelli-
gent at that moment. "I guess I should be flattered,
but I can't shake the feeling that I'm just stumbling
through this place, making one mistake after
another."

"Nobody expects perfection from you, Alice,"
Amari reassured me. "Not even Jacques. All that
matters is that you keep pushing yourself to learn and
grow. If you do that, everything else will fall into
place."

"Well, as long as you're not expecting perfection . . . I'll do what I can."

"Sometimes," Amari said gently, her words
pulling me back from the edge of anxiety, "it's not
about being the strongest or the most skilled. It's
about having the courage to face your fears and stand
up for what's right."

I sighed, considering her words. Maybe she had a
point – maybe all I needed was the courage to face
whatever horrors awaited me. But one thing was for
sure: if I wanted to help her and her people, I'd have
to dig deep—like, *insanely* deep, and find my inner
warrior.

"Okay," I agreed, even though doubt was still
lingering in my voice. "I'll give it everything I've got."

"I appreciate any help I can get. You were born to
wield the Vorpal Sword, Alice. You will drive back
the darkness, and restore light and hope to Wonderland once more."

I shook my head. "It's just . . . it's such a tall
order. Even with your help. Even with Jack training

me. Roxanne seems so powerful. And from what I understand, she's had centuries to strengthen her magic."

Suddenly I shot Amari a skeptical look. Something wasn't adding up.

"How exactly does that work, when you and Roxanne are human? How can this cycle of her going insane, and you summoning Alices have gone on for centuries? Don't you get old? Don't you die?"

"We do grow old . . . and we will someday die," she said. "Time works differently in Wonderland. It's not like your world or an afterworld or an underworld. It simply *is*. And right now, Wonderland is woefully out of balance."

"Has your sister always been like this?" I asked. "Is there a reason why she always goes off the deep end?"

Amari sighed, her face shadowed with sadness. "It began when we were children. We were close once, Roxanne and I. The best of friends. Although she's my elder sister, I was always more gifted with the magical powers of imagination than she was. She became incredibly jealous of my natural talents."

While I ate the rest of my cupcake, I listened attentively, trying to imagine what it must have been like for Amari to watch her sister turn into the psycho bitch that everyone hated. She gazed out at the frozen garden, her kind eyes becoming more distant as she went on.

"I tried to share my knowledge and skills with her, but her jealousy and selfishness drove us apart.

As we grew older, Roxanne's obsession with power also grew. She wanted to control everything – not just the Kingdom of Hearts and Roses, but all of Wonderland. Her ambition eventually consumed her, turning her into the cruel and merciless Red Queen she is today. By the time I realized how dangerous she was becoming, it was too late. She'd learned how to summon the Jabberwocky to do her bidding . . . and she made him kill our parents."

My jaw fell open at the shocking revelation, leaving me speechless.

"After the King and Queen were dead, Roxanne seized control of Wonderland, claiming it as her birthright since she was the eldest. She banished me and my court to this frozen realm."

Amari motioned to the immense beauty of the ice garden that surrounded us. "Even in defeat, there are lessons to learn. Even in pain, there is beauty. That's why I renamed this place the Kingdom of Diamonds and Ice. It's harder to survive here, but it makes us incredibly resilient and strong."

I stared at her, stunned. "You really don't mind the cold?"

She smiled gently, shaking her head. "I cherish it. The further away I am from my poisonous sister, the stronger my magic is. But I can't control her all by myself. That's why I keep summoning Alices to help me bring balance to our world."

"Is there any hope for your sister?" I cautiously asked, wondering if redemption was possible for someone as twisted as Roxanne.

"I wish I knew the answer to that question, Alice," Amari replied, her voice tinged with sadness. "I've tried countless times to reach out to her, to remind her of the love we once shared. But each time, she only grows more distant and vengeful. My greatest hope is to somehow bring peace to my sister's tortured soul. Each time, I hope Roxanne has learned her lesson at last. Each time, I am disappointed."

I toyed with the cupcake wrapper in my fingers, folding it over and tearing at the edges. The pressure of my newfound calling was bearing down on me like a thousand tons of ice. But more than that, was the knowledge of Callister and Ransom's plan to be done with the Red Queen for good.

Even if it meant her death.

Something told me that Amari wasn't in on that particular plan.

"Amari," I began, "don't you ever get tired of repeating this cycle? Of watching your sister go insane and forcing you to bring new Alices to Wonderland, only to watch your people suffer the same dark fate? Have you ever considered putting a permanent end to all of this?"

Her eyes widened in surprise, as if the thought had never occurred to her before. "Putting a permanent end to the cycle?" she murmured, a ripple of unease passing over her otherwise serene expression. "This is my destiny, Alice. It's my duty to right the wrongs of my sister. It's what I was born to do."

"Destiny or not," I countered, my voice holding a subtle edge, "aren't you tired of constantly fighting with your sister and seeing all the pain she causes? Aren't you sick of watching Wonderland fall into ruin time and time again? There's got to be another way – a better way."

For a moment, Amari looked lost in thought, her gaze distant and unfocused. The ethereal ice garden around us seemed to hold its breath, as though awaiting her response. Finally, she shook her head gently, her tight purple curls swaying with the motion.

"I've been doing this for so long, Alice," she admitted, her voice tinged with sadness. "Perhaps I have become too complacent, too accepting of the way things are . . . of how they've always been. But what choice do I have? It's either this or surrendering to Roxanne's darkness completely."

"Then we'll have to find another way," I declared, my determination unwavering. "I'm sure we can break this cycle for good. We just need to think outside the box . . . come up with a plan that'll turn the tables on Roxanne once and for all."

Amari hesitated, clearly taken aback by my boldness. Maybe it was because I already knew about the plan to kill Roxanne. Or maybe it was because I hadn't spent a lifetime trapped in this twisted game of cat-and-mouse – but I could see the possibilities, the potential for change. In my mind, it was as clear as day.

"Perhaps you're right," Amari admitted after a beat, her eyes meeting mine with renewed hope. "Maybe we can find a way to end this cycle and free

Wonderland from Roxanne's grip. But it won't be easy. Are you honestly prepared to face the challenges and darkness that lie ahead?"

"Not yet, but I will be," I replied with a wry grin as we stood up to leave. "Bring it on."

CHAPTER

SIX

ALICE

"Mornin' Jack," I chirped with a ridiculously bright
and cheerful smile as I strolled into the courtyard.
Not only was I on time, but I was dressed in an even
sluttier outfit than yesterday. I hadn't left a single
damn thing to the imagination.

I still had my hair in a high pony, but I'd traded
the leotard for hot pink, butt-lifting yoga pants with
deep ruching that dove right into my crack, showing
off my round ass cheeks. My top was white, thin, and
mostly made of straps. It barely held my tits in place,
and left my stomach completely exposed. I'd only
been in the frozen practice space for a minute, and
my nips were already as hard as pencil erasers.

I couldn't wait until I started sweating. My
skimpy top would practically become transparent.
Since Jack already loathed me, I was determined to
make him hate his job even more.

The light of dawn was just spilling through the

huge, arched, frosted windows, protecting the undead, gorgeous asshat from any killer rays.

He'd traded the heavy metal armor from yesterday for a muscle-hugging getup made of sleek black leather and metal buckles that matched his long platinum hair. He stopped arranging the agility ladder on the icy floor and looked at me like I'd lost my damn mind.

Then he scowled.

Finally, he looked away.

I got the impression he didn't approve of my outfit.

Not at all.

That only made me grin wider.

I chose that moment to take a casual gulp of the pumpkin spice latte in my hand.

"Breakfast," I explained as I joined him, then tapped the Starbucks logo on the cup. This PSL might've been the most impressive thing I'd imagined since arriving in Wonderland.

Jack caught a whiff of the triple shots doused in oat milk and whipped cream and wrinkled his nose, clearly unimpressed.

Good.

Fuck this stuck-up, arrogant jerk.

After the outright abuse I'd taken from him the day before, I decided nothing would piss off the White Knight more than proving just how little he'd gotten under my skin.

I put one hand on my hip, then bent down and

set the Starbucks cup beside the rope ladder lying on the ground between us.

"Hey, I know I still owe you like, two-hundred and ninety-three minutes of running, or whatever. Do you want me to start doing laps now, or wait until we're done with our lesson?"

Jack's red eyes widened as he looked at me with a mixture of surprise and confusion. The corners of his lips curved up, hinting at a smile that never quite materialized.

"You remembered the exact number of minutes you owe me?"

"Of course I remembered! I'm more than just a hot piece of ass who's gonna save Wonderland, you know." I shot an exaggerated wink at him, feeling a sudden flutter in my chest at the possibility of Jack being impressed by anything I did.

I quickly shoved it aside.

I didn't need—or want—his approval for anything.

"Very well," Jack replied with a subtle nod, maintaining his air of nobility. "Start running."

I set a pace that was fast enough to keep him from summoning more of the abyssal hounds, yet slow enough to maintain in case he decided to make me run for more than half an hour.

While I ran laps around the courtyard, I did everything I could to ignore the douche canoe with the body of a Roman god who was setting up some kind of obstacle course. There was a set of balance beams, all at different heights. One of the walls had been covered in gigantic mirrors.

Being that the courtyard was made of white stone covered in frost, Jack's dark silhouette stuck out like a sore thumb. He stood tall and regal, with an air of nobility, but he was like a black hole, sucking the light into that leather armor . . . armor that just happened to be perfectly molded to his hard, swollen muscles. I mean, every fucking ripple was accounted for. It clung to him like a second skin.

Look away, Alice, I scolded myself as I ran. *Look the fuck away from him!*

I imagined a pair of wireless earbuds, and within seconds they were blasting my favorite workout mix into my head. My brain was filled only with the beat of the music and the sensation of my feet hitting the ground. All I had to focus on was trying not to fall.

I never imagined that my life would lead me here, to this beautiful, frozen Kingdom of Diamonds and Ice. I clenched my jaw as I landed one sneaker in front of the other, nodding in time to the beat. This was my reality now—no more Hollywood afterparties, no more designer dresses, and no more getting dragged and bullied on social media for being a dumbass.

All I had to concern myself with was mastering the cold, hard steel of the Vorpal Sword and bearing the weight of a kingdom's fate on my shoulders.

Suddenly I collided with a wall of black leather.

I let out a scream before coming back to my senses.

Jack was standing in front of me.

His piercing red eyes assessed me with a mix of curiosity and skepticism, like I was a puzzle he was trying to solve. The cold air of the training courtyard bit into my skin, but it was nothing compared to the chill his gaze sent through me.

"Alice!"

He snapped his fingers and my earbuds disappeared. "Enough running for now," he announced while pressing my practice sword into my hand. "It's time to correct your shoddy footwork."

Even though I was panting from all the running, I nodded and gave him a thumbs-up. "Sounds great!" I huffed with fake enthusiasm. "Where do we start?"

Without missing a beat, Jack began coaching me on a series of drills using the agility ladder. It was basically like playing hopscotch on ice. He walked slow circles around me, his arms crossed, watching me with an intensity that made the air feel heavier.

"Begin with the basic one-two step," he instructed, his voice a commanding echo in the cavernous room. "Focus on precision, not speed."

I nodded and started moving my feet in and out of the squares. It felt awkward, the sword a cumbersome companion in this dance of agility.

"No," Jack interrupted, his tone sharp. "You're not a clodhopping peasant at a fair. You're a warrior. Do it again. This time with elegance and grace."

I stopped, suppressing a sigh. "Yeah, grace and elegance have never been my strong suit," I joked.

93

"Then make them your strong suit," Jack replied coolly. "Your life may depend on it."

I rolled my eyes. "Do you ever laugh?"

One of Jack's eyebrows lifted as he studied me.

"No. Now do the two-step until you've shown at least a modicum of grace."

I tried again, this time attempting to channel the elegant movements of a ballerina. It felt slightly better, but still far from the fluidity that Jack embodied.

"Better," Jack conceded, although his voice was devoid of praise. "But don't let your guard down. The Red Queen won't show mercy."

I got back into starting position and lifted my sword, my grip firm even though I was trembling with fatigue.

"Now, integrate the side-step weave. Keep in mind that each movement is a potential dodge in combat."

I moved through the ladder, adding the side-step weave. It was a challenge to keep the rhythm and not tangle my feet.

"Imagine each square is a trap on the battlefield," Jack said, circling closer around me like a silver lion about to pounce. The wild, outdoorsy scent of leather and balsam drifted near my nose, making my focus wobble. "Each misstep could be fatal. Precision, Alice. Precision."

"Easy for you to say," I retorted, trying to keep up with the footwork while ignoring his invigorating scent. "I'm sure you've had a few extra centuries to practice compared to me."

"A fair point," he admitted, his voice softening slightly. "But you have the potential to learn quickly. Now, add an offensive movement. Strike as you step."

Balancing the footwork with the sword strikes felt as logical as trying to find valet parking at a Taco Bell. I flailed around and fucked up my steps, then whacked the side of my leg with my sword before slipping on the ice and falling on my ass.

Stifling a groan, Jack halted me with a raised hand. "Please . . . stop whatever this is that you're doing. Step aside and observe."

He demonstrated the sequence with the Vorpal Sword, his movements a fluid dance of lethal elegance. Every step, every strike was purposeful and precise. It was poetry in motion to watch his beautiful, powerful body move.

For a moment, I forgot to breathe.

"Now you try," he said, taking a step back. "Mimic what you just saw me do. Feel the rhythm . . . feel the flow of the movement through your body."

I took a deep breath and started again, trying to copy Jack's seamless combination of elegance and combat. My feet stumbled and my strikes were unco-ordinated, but I refused to give up.

Jack watched for a few moments before stepping in again.

"You're still too focused on your speed," he pointed out. "Focus on your precision. Slow down and concentrate on each movement. Speed will come in time."

"What if I don't have a lot of time?" I argued.

Jack replied with an unapologetic shrug.

"Then expect mass casualties. If you can't hit your target, it won't matter how fast you are. Now slow down and do it properly."

I nodded and tried again, this time taking as long as I needed with each step and strike. It felt awkward at first, but gradually my movements became smoother and more fluid.

"Better," Jack said approvingly. "But don't forget to keep your guard up while striking."

I lifted my elbow a few inches.

"Like this?"

"No." He sheathed his sword and stepped over to me.

Fuck. He was close.

Like . . . *really* close.

Close enough to feel his soft breath on my bare shoulder.

"Close your eyes," he said, his voice low and serious as he curled his hand around my upper arm. "I want to show you something."

I hesitated for a moment before closing them, but he was my mentor and I was his apprentice. I did as I was told, although my heart was thumping wildly in my chest. What the hell was he about to show me that required me to close my eyes?

Be cool! Act normal! Don't let him know that deep down, I think his leather armor would look a lot sexier on the floor next to my bed. Or maybe he could leave it on. And definitely don't let him know that he smells fucking amazing.

I felt Jack shift behind me, then a soft rustling sound as he moved something nearby. Suddenly, a cold, hard object was resting against my throat– the tip of a blade. My eyes flew open in surprise and I immediately started to pull away.

"Don't move," Jack warned in a low voice, holding me tight. "Just feel."

My heart pounded in fear and strange excitement as I waited for whatever surprise Jack had in store for me. Was he going to slice open my neck and drink my blood? Was he waiting for me to scream? Was this some kind of mental resilience drill, or torture preparedness training?

"Do you feel that?" Jack asked gently, nudging the blade slightly so that it grazed over my skin.

"Yeah, I fucking feel it," I replied breathlessly.

"That's the potential of your power," he continued. "But you won't possess it until you can wield a sword with both speed and precision. I will accept nothing less."

"Do you talk to all of your Alices this way, or just me?"

A low, amused hum rose from his chest before he lowered his sword and put it away.

"Just you."

I narrowed my eyes at him. "I'm serious!"

"So am I," he said, not letting go of my arm. "Children are eager to learn, and quick to imagine

themselves capable of achieving anything they set
their mind to. The young Alices I've trained only
needed an afternoon or two of instruction. Adoles-
cents and adults think they already know all there is
to know. They can easily take years to train."

Years? I swallowed hard as I digested what he'd
just told me.

"Um . . . about that . . . I don't think I have years
to learn this."

"It will take as long as it takes," came Jack's
cryptic reply. Still holding my arm in one hand, he
took my wrist in the other, holding me in a way that
was gentle, but firm.

I wonder if he'd hold me like that if he was fu—

"Your blade is a part of your body."

Oh holy hell . . . he was so strong . . . so fucking
strong. And now he was making my body move while
I turned to putty. I watched with a blank expression
as he manipulated my arm into a graceful arc. "Treat
your weapon as if it were your hand or your foot. Let
it move as one."

The sound of his voice, the tone of it, sent a
shudder through my core. Biting back a gasp, I
relaxed and let my body move at his every command.

He abruptly let go of me, taking that wild,
woodsy, alpine scent along with him. I blinked and
saw him standing beside me on the agility ladder.

"I'll do it with you. Watch yourself in the mirror.
Do what I do."

*Welp—so much for avoiding eye contact after all
that touchy-feely stuff.*

I studied our reflections in the mirror as he unsheathed the Vorpal Sword. Together, we went through the drill, doing the sequence in slow motion, moving simultaneously, doing it again and again. Seeing the two of us side by side would've been hilarious if I wasn't concentrating so hard.

Here I was, dressed like a slutty gym rat, while he looked like the star of the latest gladiator movie.

By some miracle, I eventually began to find a rhythm, a harmony between footwork and swordplay.

"That's it," Jack encouraged, still going through every motion with me. "Now faster. Don't sacrifice precision for speed."

We continued, Jack coaching me through the intricacies of each movement. With every attack, our swords met with a resounding clang that echoed off the icy walls. His critiques were sharp but fair, pushing me to try harder. Every observation he made was followed by the one word I was starting to hate—

"Again."

As I ran through my drills over and over again, I realized this was more than just checking off a box on my list of how to learn sword fighting. This footwork was being seared into the muscle memory of my brain and my body until I could do it as easily as fastening a button or spotting a fake Birkin bag.

"Good," Jack finally said. "Now let's put it into practice. En garde."

A blur of shining white silver flashed in front of me as Jack lunged forward, knocking my sword out of my hands and onto the icy floor.

"Hey! I wasn't ready!"

"I know." Jack's voice cut through my thoughts of indignation, sharp as the sword he was now holding at my chest. "Your enemies won't wait for you to be ready."

"Duly noted," I shot back. "I thought you'd be above taking a cheap shot."

Jack shook his head, then lowered his weapon.

"I'll take any shot my enemy is foolish enough to allow." I watched as he slipped the toe of his boot under my sword, hiked it up into the air, caught it, and handed it over to me. "You would be wise to do the same."

He lunged at me again, his movements a blur of black and silver. I barely managed to block his strike. The impact of our swords rang in my ears, jarring my arms so hard that it knocked the sword from my hands.

I dove for it, but Jack's boot had the blade pinned to the ground. The cold, sharp tip of his sword brushed against my throat.

"Dead," he gloated from above. "Do it again."

I wrenched free, retrieving my sword.

This time I lasted longer, reading Jack's moves better. His strikes came fast as a viper, but there it was—a moment's hesitation. I grinned and launched a flurry of blows, driving him back.

A brief look of satisfaction crossed his face before he rallied. Our fight turned intense, bordering on the edge of violence. I gasped as his sword grazed my forearm, which was as cold as his fingertips had felt earlier.

Jack's eyes glowed, and for a second I glimpsed the predator beneath his noble facade. My heart raced—but I didn't know if it was out of fear or something more dangerous.

"You're welcome to put on armor at any time," he said, not even the slightest bit winded.

"But I won't need it, will I?" I said with a mock curtsy. "Not with as good of a teacher as you."

Jack's lips quirked, and I ran at him full speed. My arms burned as I blocked his blows, struggling to keep up with his vampiric speed and strength. Sweat began to bead on my forehead, a stark contrast to the icy ground beneath my feet.

But I wouldn't give up.

I couldn't.

Suddenly I was lying on my back. I didn't know how, but it didn't matter. All that mattered was that I was still holding onto my sword. I immediately pointed it at Jack's chest.

"Good. You're learning," he said, circling me. I could hear a hint of genuine approval in his voice, and I felt a surge of pride at his praise. He motioned with his hand for me to come at him once more. "But you'll have to do a *lot* better if you want to defeat the Red Queen. Again."

The rhythmic sound of our swords clashing filled the courtyard, each strike sending a burst of adrenaline surging through me as his sword pushed me to my limits. Each swing and thrust forced me to adapt, to move in ways I never thought possible. I could feel muscles I didn't know existed screaming in protest.

Thanks to my regular spin class, I was no stranger to physical exertion, but this was a whole new level. This felt like survival. With each parry, each dodge, I was learning not just to fight, but to keep alive the hope of a world teetering on the brink of darkness.

No pressure or anything.

Just the fate of the world resting in my weak-ass hands.

Jack's next round of strikes came faster, more aggressive, more complex, as if testing how far he could push me. I sidestepped, barely avoiding the blade. My heart was pounding in my chest, a wild rhythm that echoed the clashes of steel on steel.

I gritted my teeth and swung at Jack again, sweat dripping down my brow. I would prove to Jack that I was worthy of being his apprentice. Each time I fell—every single bruise and scrape—only fueled my determination.

I wouldn't break.

Other than a few water breaks for me, we sparred all morning and into the early afternoon. On the low beam, on the medium, along the agility ladder, our bodies constantly moving in tandem . . . push, pull . . . push, pull. All of it was part of our dance.

Our training was like a seductive tango, each move calculated and precise. Bodies bending to one side, then the other. Jack's blade slicing through the air with deadly accuracy, teasing my skin with an icy touch . . . like a deadly lover's caress. With every parry and thrust, our bodies moved in perfect harmony, advancing and retreating from each other in a fierce battle.

I couldn't help but notice how Jack's muscles rippled under his leather armor with each powerful thrust and parry; how his hypnotic red eyes lit up with excitement on the rare occasion when we managed to trap each other in a stalemate. The way our gazes locked when our swords met. The way his nose was just a few inches from mine.

It was intoxicating.

Addictive.

And I found myself wanting more.

"You're not that bad," he said as he stopped and took a step back. He sheathed his sword, making me wonder if we were done for the day. I watched his arm muscles bulge and flex as he reached behind his head to tie back his hair.

I tried not to stare, but holy shit—he was a beautiful creature. Such a perfectly shaped mouth . . . so many hard, sharp lines in his jaw, along his nose. No wonder some other vampire had decided to preserve this perfect specimen of man until the end of time.

As Jack smoothed his hair back with his fingers and tied it low at the back of his neck, every movement of his chiseled face had me mesmerized. He was beautiful, powerful, and moved in ways that had me thinking less about practice, and more about his raw masculinity.

Watching him do something so common and mundane made him seem almost . . . human.

Almost . . . vulnerable . . . a stark contrast to his usual cold exterior. His eyes flicked up at me and I gulped as if I'd been caught doing something I shouldn't have.

"Your parry could use some work."

God help me. His voice was smooth as silk.

"Oh yeah?" I countered, faking offense. "Maybe you can show me what you have in mind?"

He stepped closer, our bodies almost touching, and guided my hand and my sword through the proper motion.

"Hold your weapon like this," he murmured, his voice barely more than a whisper, as his lips hovered dangerously close to my ear. I could feel the coolness of his breath against my neck, making me shudder involuntarily. My breath hitched in my throat, the scent of him intoxicating my senses.

"Got it," I replied, trying to mask the sound of my shaky voice. I quickly pulled away and took a defensive stance, desperate to regain some semblance of composure.

I held my ground, readying myself for his inevitable attack. He easily outmaneuvered my parry, his movements fluid and graceful like a predatory cat stalking its prey. It was both fascinating and infuriating to watch him in action, especially given how effortlessly he seemed to anticipate my every move.

"Focus, Alice," he reminded me. This time his voice was more stern, but I found myself enjoying it. There was something about Jack – the way he held himself, the frustrated way he looked at me – that made me want to push him even further, to see how far we could go before one of us fell apart.

And although I knew it was dangerous, I couldn't help wanting to taste the darkness that lurked beneath his refined exterior.

Our swords clashed again. A shower of sparks erupted from the point of contact. The muscles in Jack's arms flexed beneath his armor, the sight momentarily distracting me.

"Alice . . . " he growled as he pushed against me. "Pay attention!"

"Sorry," I muttered through gritted teeth, forcing myself to concentrate on the task at hand. But it was hard – so hard – when all I could think about was what he did at night when he wasn't here training me.

Was he at parties, seducing members of the White Queen's court into letting him drink from them? Did he have a girlfriend? A boyfriend? One of each? Did he sleep in the nude? Did he have a dog? Maybe a pet wolf? Did he drink wine?

Did he *really* never laugh?

"Alice!"

Two smoldering red eyes were holding me captive, and it took a moment for me to realize the cool sensation on my jaw was his hand holding my chin. The sheer intensity of his gaze made my breath catch in my throat.

"Your mind seems to be elsewhere," he said in a low growl. It was the kind of growl that made the hairs on the back of my neck immediately stand up.

"Perhaps if you paid more attention, you'd stand a chance."

I blinked at him, speechless.

Meanwhile, my inner monologue wouldn't shut up.

Perhaps if you weren't so fucking gorgeous and mysterious, I could concentrate better.

His eyes sparkled like rubies as they bored into mine, and in that moment I would've let him do anything he wanted to me. He clenched his jaw enough for me to see the muscles feather beneath his flawless skin.

But as he held my chin, I could feel his hand shaking.

Not a lot.

But it was *definitely* shaking.

"We're done for today," Jack said quietly, and abruptly let go of me. He stepped away from me and sheathed his sword.

"Are you sure? I'm sorry I wasn't paying attention. Let's try it again."

"No." Glancing over his shoulder, Jack looked up at the windows. They were streaked with orange and purple . . . the colors of approaching twilight. "It's late. We'll pick up where we left off in the morning."

"Okay." Even though he was right about it getting late, I couldn't help feeling like I'd done something wrong . . . like a line had been crossed.

"You did well today," he mused. Then his eyes darkened. "I'll have to go harder on you tomorrow."

A thrill ran through me at his words.

At his praise.

At his threat.

"I can take it," I said breathlessly as I headed for the door.

Jack's expression turned predatory. "Can you now? We shall see."

CHAPTER

SEVEN

JACK

The freshly fallen snow smothered the sound of my boots as I ventured into the woods, searching for the only thing that would quell my inhuman thirst. Snowflakes fell against my cheeks, each one of them a frozen kiss, but I paid them no mind.

This was the best time to hunt . . . when the clouds were low and heavy . . . when the snow fell so fast and thick that it muffled every sound I made . . . and every sound around me.

Prey would be harder to find, but I enjoyed the challenge.

And right now, I needed the distraction.

Ever since Alice's arrival, I'd been ensnared in a battle I never anticipated. One that waged deep within the caverns of my undead heart, where my vampire nature dwells like a caged beast, thirsting for something beyond blood.

Her.

Training her was a torment. Each swing of her

sword sent a pulse through me, an electric jolt that stirred something primal. It was my duty to watch her move, to study the determination etched in every one of her strained muscles. Sometimes it felt as if she danced just for me, unwittingly weaving a spell I was becoming more and more desperate to resist.

Today, our session teetered on the edge of disaster. Every time she lunged forward, her scent engulfed me—a mix of sweat, sensuality, and something uniquely Alice. My instincts were distracting me, urging me to close the distance, to taste the pulse that fluttered in her neck. So many times I almost succumbed, the monster within mere seconds from breaking free.

Somehow, I managed to step back, cloaking my turmoil with a mask of indifference.

But how much longer could I keep it up?

I pursed my lips as I reflected on my newest apprentice. I'd trained so many Alices that I'd almost lost count . . .

Alicia, a bossy little brunette from Spain.

Alicja, a tiny wisp of a girl from Poland.

Alis, the ferocious Welsh fighter who seemed born to wield the Vorpal Sword.

Alizeh from Persia, who slayed the Jabberwocky on her first attempt. I wasn't supposed to have favorites, but she was certainly up there.

But this newest Alice . . .

I shook my head, then blew out a breath in frustration.

It wasn't that she was older than any of my other

young apprentices by more than a decade. It wasn't that she lacked the level of imagination that came so naturally to young children. It wasn't even the knowledge that she'd been born into wealth. I myself came from a noble family and I lacked for nothing growing up.

But I was taught the duty and responsibility that came with such status. As the eldest son of a marquis, I was a prominent figure in my community, whereas this Alice seemed to have been taught nothing but the hedonistic pursuits of her own pleasure. Whatever privilege she was born into was squandered.

Yes . . . that was most likely my source of frustration.

At twenty-six, the same exact age as this Alice, I was the heir to my family's vast estates. I had the duty of managing the land, the crops, and the servants. I settled disputes among our tenants when my younger brothers could not. I trained armies of men to be of service to our king when my uncles could not.

I hosted tournaments, feasts, and other social events, not only as entertainment for the people of our city, but also as a way of building alliances with other regional diplomats. I weighed in on local politics and trade, oversaw merchant ventures, maritime interests, and trade negotiations.

I had a wife and four children. Three boys and one precious little girl. I buried all of them when the Black Death came. There wasn't time to mourn them. I was too busy digging graves for my brothers and their families. For my cousins and their families.

One by one, brick by brick, the House des Diamants fell, along with half the population of my city. I no longer hosted diplomatic feasts. Instead, I helped organize and dig mass graves. I no longer walked to the markets with my family, carrying my daughter on my shoulders. I walked past piles of rotting corpses lying in the streets. I didn't stop and speak with my friends and neighbors. They were all covered with maggots and flies, vultures pecking at their bodies, as they shriveled and putrified in the summer heat.

At six and twenty years of age, I did all of this and more.

Every day.

For over two *years*.

What did this Alice of the same age have to offer, aside from the ability to dress like a common whore and drink to excess and complain about how difficult her life was?

She knew absolutely *nothing* of how difficult life could be.

Most of my young Alices knew at least that much. I recalled one of them arriving in Wonderland so malnourished that I refused to train her for an entire fortnight. Watching her eat her fill had been so satisfying . . .

Unlike my current Alice.

She'd been born into privilege yet remained willfully ignorant.

"Why must she be so vexing?" I muttered under

my breath, knowing that my voice wouldn't carry far in the falling snow.

Just then I caught a movement in the corner of my eye. I spun, ready to strike. It was only a rabbit. Not much sport in taking such a small creature. I stared deep into its glittering black eyes.

"Lucky for you I'm not that desperate. You'd better run while you can."

The rabbit's nose twitched at me in understanding before it darted away into the underbrush.

With quiet grace, I continued walking through the darkness, careful not to disturb the serenity of the forest. The wind began to pick up, sending my cloak billowing around me like a ghostly shadow.

Suddenly, there it was. The faint scent of a deer in the near distance, its warm, earthy aroma calling to the primal hunter within me.

My pulse quickened, adrenaline surging as I zeroed in on my target. It was a doe, camouflaged by the dense cover of pine trees that brushed against the low clouds above.

But it didn't matter if I couldn't see her.

I could smell her.

It wouldn't be long until she was in my arms, thrashing desperately, fighting to live.

Let the chase begin.

My bloodlust led me by the nose through the snow-dusted trees, my boots barely making a sound as I quickly found tracks of my prey. My mouth began to water in anticipation of the hot, metallic taste of fresh blood. She would be more than enough for me to drink my fill. I ran my tongue along my fangs as I caught sight of the doe in a small clearing among the trees.

In one fluid motion, I leapt from tree to tree, closing in on my target. I landed gracefully behind the doe in a surge of speed, pinning her to the ground beneath my weight. Her legs thrashed about wildly, but I held fast.

The warmth of her body against mine, and her struggle to live was intoxicating.

This very moment was what I lived for.

My existence was not much different than the wild animals of the forest . . . or the jungle . . . or the plains—

Kill or be killed.

Hunt or become the hunted.

Of all the deadly creatures in this forest, I was the apex predator.

The doe thrashed and bucked as I sank my teeth deep into her jugular. My mouth closed around the wound, and I drank freely and deeply, drawing her life force into me. Warm blood filled my mouth and gushed down my throat, licking at my insides like a lover's tongue . . . satisfying a thirst that would never truly be quenched.

The thrashing slowed as the doe accepted her fate. Her heartbeat thudded in my ears, urging me to take my fill. Enormous brown eyes blinked in under-standing as she surrendered her life to me.

She had just learned the lesson that I'd spent my entire life teaching—

Every living thing must someday die.

In the distance, I could hear the familiar hunt calls of wolves, foxes, and birds of prey. I swallowed one last mouthful of precious blood, then let her neck slip out of my hands and into the snow. I knew that after I'd satisfied my own hunger, this creature's body would continue to feed many more.

I wiped my mouth and headed straight for the castle. My intent was to locate Queen Amari and update her on Alice's progress in training, as I did with all my apprentices, then retire back to my chambers.

I stopped by her private library, but she wasn't there. She wasn't in the throne room, either. Perhaps she was still at dinner.

As I neared the entrance to the Great Hall, my ears were met with a cacophony of laughter. Normally I would've avoided such a crowd, but I'd just fed and my belly was full. There was no safer time for me to be among the living, aside from early hours of the morning.

I took off my gloves, then stopped in front of a nearby mirror and studied my reflection. My skin was warm and flushed with the doe's blood, making me look practically human. The snowflakes had melted, leaving my hair damp. Only a small dab of red lingered near the corner of my mouth. I licked it away, smoothed my hair back, then peered around the massive wooden doors, searching for my queen.

My eyes darted around, surveying the room within seconds. There was no sign of Amari. I noticed Ransom sitting at a table, and a swell of relief washed over me. When I saw the extent of his injuries upon arrival, I wasn't sure that he'd be able to keep his wings. From what I could tell, he'd made a full recovery from the Red Queen's poison arrows and was celebrating with Callister, Chess, and Hatter.

And Alice.

Irritation immediately clouded my vision as I observed the number of empty wine bottles sitting in front of her. My jaw clenched at the loud, carefree way she laughed, as if my queen wasn't depending on her to save the people of Wonderland.

Very well . . . if Alice wanted to stay up late carousing and drinking, so be it.

I would make her pay dearly for it in the morning.

Debating whether or not I should advise my queen to summon a new Alice, I tried to slip away unnoticed. Just then, Hatter caught my gaze.

"Jack! Hey Jack! Look who's out of the infirmary!" he shouted through the Great Hall, beckoning me over with a flourish. The chatter in the room died down as dozens upon dozens of courtiers stopped what they were doing and looked at me.

I wasn't exactly known for making social calls.

Suddenly Chess appeared in front of me out of thin air. His grin was mischievous and wide as he clapped a hand on my shoulder. "We're celebrating Ransom's recovery. Come join us!"

With a sigh of resignation, I followed him into the

room. That was the problem with having such manners be seared into my mind since birth. As I approached the table, Chess found an empty chair and shoved it between Hatter's place and Alice's, then motioned for me to sit.

I did not sit.

"The honorable White Knight, Jacques des Diamants, or Jack of Diamonds, you honor us with your presence!" Hatter declared with a drunken flourish. He patted the chair cushion with a mad glint in his mismatched eyes. "Have some wine and make merry with us!"

"You fool," Callister scoffed from across the table. He sat beneath a thick cloud of dark blue smoke. He reloaded his hookah and the smoke turned pale pink. "The White Knight doesn't make merry."

"That tracks," Alice added, giving me a condescending once-over. "He told me earlier today that he never laughs."

I narrowed my eyes at her. I detested hearing her speak about me as if I wasn't standing right beside her.

"So what if he doesn't laugh or make merry? He's not here to entertain you," Ransom said with an air of authority. His demon eyes were glowing gold with incredible vitality as they turned in my direction. "Jack, if you would stay and have a drink with us, it would be an honor."

I mulled over the invitation in my head, then slowly removed my cloak and jacket. I begrudgingly sat down next to Alice, immediately aware of just how close she was. At least she was dressed more modestly. A sharp contrast from her outfit this morning, the shapeless sweater she now wore seemed to swallow her whole, from her wrists to her neck.

Despite my frustration with her, there was no denying her beauty, which only served to irritate me more.

But the scent that wafted from her . . .

Dear gods, it threatened to tear me apart.

The fragrance was tantaliz-ing . . . fresh . . . tart . . . sweet . . . crisp.

My mouth began to water.

I was no longer here at this table in the Great Hall.

I was no longer in the White Queen's castle.

I wasn't even in Wonderland.

I was back on one of my family's most remote estates. The plague had ravaged the land far and wide for over two years, taking so many lives that there weren't enough people left to plant and harvest crops. There was no grain to make bread. Everyone blessed to survive now had to deal with famine and crime as our new daily reality.

With most of my family dead, I'd left the city and gone deeper into the countryside to live off of my family's land. I spent my days fishing and hunting and eating as many apples as I wanted from our vast orchards.

In fact, the very last thing I ate as a mortal man was an apple.

So when Alice tossed her freshly washed hair

over her shoulder and bathed me in the scent of freshly cut apples, it was all I could do not lean close and demand she give me a taste.

I watched as her chest rose and fell under her oversized garment, her breasts shifting with each breath.

Why did she have to be so damned beautiful?

And so off limits?

I couldn't stop looking.

"Jack?"

I blinked, suddenly transported back to the table in Wonderland. My gaze slid down to my young apprentice.

"What is it?"

"Did you want red or white?" she asked innocently, motioning to the wine glass in her hand.

"Red. I'll pour it myself."

Too late. She was already filling the glass with one of the half-dozen bottles scattered around the table.

"Thank you." I took the glass from her, careful to not let our fingers come into contact.

I knew she was going to be trouble.

I simply hadn't anticipated how much.

The wine's deep, rich aroma filled my nostrils, but it paled in comparison to Alice's scent. I raised my glass, and the others followed suit.

All except for my apprentice, who lifted a glass of sliced lemons dancing in semi-transparent liquid.

Apparently wine wasn't strong enough for her.

"Here's to Ransom's miraculous recovery," I

declared with genuine appreciation. We all clinked
our glasses together before taking a drink in his
honor. The wine was among the finest in the kingdom, but it would never compare to the blood I had
sated myself on earlier.

"Thank you, Jack," Ransom said between sips of
his wine. "Really, it's good to have you join us."

Chess grinned even wider. "You should let loose
like this more often."

I hummed in mock amusement as Alice finished
gulping her drink and set it down, half empty.

"I don't know if I could keep pace with you," I
said, eyeing her beverage with disapproval as it
refilled itself. "What's in your glass? Vodka? Gin?"

Alice's eyes pinned onto mine, and the rhythm of
her heartbeat sped up, drumming from her chest
directly into my ears.

"It's water," she deadpanned. "Some of us have to
get up early in the morning."

Still staring at me, she stabbed a forkful of roast
carrots off her plate and slipped them past her soft
lips, letting them rest on her pink tongue in such a
way that it made my cock take notice and grow jealous. Then she turned her attention back to Ransom
and Chess, who were chatting about antidotes for
poison.

I was so beside myself that I almost didn't pick up
on the fact that Alice was now suggesting Ransom
should work with Queen Amari to build up a surplus
of treatments for the poison used by the Red Queen's
army.

Was this the same woman?

Where was the spoiled, self-indulgent brat from only a few days ago? What happened to the confounding, exasperating, lazy little layabout I'd been presented with?

And why did she have to smell so fucking delicious?

I finished my glass of wine in one swallow, watching it refill on my command. It was going to take a lot more wine to drown out the scent of such forbidden fruit.

Meanwhile, Alice and Ransom were now discussing military strategy. She kept referring to something called 'the Game of Thrones,' a game which I'd never heard of nor played, but I was quite familiar with some of the methods she was suggesting.

The more Alice spoke of naval ambushes using magical fire and building a ballista capable of injuring the Jabberwocky enough for her to kill him, the more I realized how little I knew about this infuriating, yet fascinating creature.

Was it possible that Queen Amari had chosen wisely after all?

"What do you think, Jack?" Alice asked as she turned to me. "Do you have any artillery that can take down the Jabberwocky? I was thinking maybe we could catch him in a huge net, and then I can stab him in the heart."

"We can discuss that in more depth later," I replied. As much as I would've enjoyed telling Alice the different options we had for such a plan, I wasn't about to broadcast them inside the Great Hall.

Too many eyes were watching us.

Too many ears were listening in.

"She's brave enough to do it," Hatter slurred. Wine sloshed out of his glass as he struggled to keep himself upright in his chair. "Did you know she almost beheaded the Red Queen? Hopefully you can teach her well enough to get the job done next time."

My ears pricked up, paying closer attention to their conversation. Out of the corner of my eye, Ransom made a throat-slashing gesture at Hatter in an attempt to silence him. It seemed he was referring to something far more dangerous than mere drunken banter.

As the Supreme Commander of the White Queen's army, any plot to kill her sister, the Red Queen, would be of great concern to me. But for now, I held my tongue, storing away the information for further investigation.

Callister blew out a puff of pink smoke and shook his head at Hatter.

"You clearly need to dip your wick in something besides warm porridge, my friend, because you're speaking nonsense."

"Oh, you should've seen it, Jack," said Hatter. "Alice and Ransom had her right there, but alas—"

"But alas, we are all out of wine," Ransom interrupted while pushing the group of empty bottles into Hatter's lap. "A true friend would go fetch some more."

Hatter's one blue eye gleamed with jealousy as he pointed a finger in Ransom's face.

"Oh . . . I see what you're up to! You're trying to get me to leave so you can all sneak away without me and fuck Alice!"

"I think he just wants more wine, Hatter," Alice said with a coy grin. She got up from her chair and pushed it back in. "Maybe now's my cue to leave. I'm going to bed with someone else tonight."

I clenched my jaw, forcing myself to remain silent despite the surge of possessiveness that gripped me.

If she wasn't fucking anyone at this table, then who was she taking to bed?

One glance around the table, and I knew I wasn't the only one thinking the same exact thing.

"Amari lent me a book about the Jabberwocky's strengths and weaknesses," she explained, tapping her temple. "I have some reading to do before I face this big bad monster I'm supposed to kill." With that, she turned on her heel and left the Great Hall, her stride confident and determined.

As I watched her walk away, I couldn't help but feel a sense of pride. She had resisted the temptation to stay up late drinking and fucking, choosing instead to focus on her training and her role in saving Wonderland.

The others stared after her, their lustful gazes lingering on her retreating, shapely form. Then they exchanged curious glances before turning their attention on me.

"That's the first time she's chosen a thick, hard book over a thick, hard cock," Ransom remarked, turning to me with a smirk. "How has she been performing for you during your private lessons, Jack? Is that why she isn't fucking any of us?"

I raised an eyebrow, slightly offended by the insinuation that I'd break my code of conduct with an apprentice.

"I do *not* fuck my students," I replied icily. "And I only share their progress with Queen Amari."

"She's not a little girl like all the others, Jack." Ransom's smirk only grew more pronounced. "She's fair game."

"Definitely game," added Hatter, before biting his lip.

"She's absolutely ripe for the fucking," said Chess. "You could have her if you wanted. We know you've noticed how irresistible she is."

"Come on, Jack," Ransom urged with a seductive grin. "We're happy to share her with you, as long as you don't keep her all to yourself. She might act a certain way in public, but behind closed doors, she's an insatiable little slut. She'd indulge you in your darkest, filthiest fantasies, and beg for more."

My eyes narrowed. "Watch your tongue, incubus, or I'll cut it from your mouth!"

"He'll just grow a new one," Hatter howled with a drunken laugh. "He's right about Alice, though. She'll let you do *anything* to her. Tie her up, stuff a gag in her mouth, fuck her in the ass, fuck all of us at once . . . "

"Enough!" I snapped, my patience at its end. "She's my apprentice! I am her mentor! Regardless of her age, I will *never* cross that line!"

"But you've thought about it," Chess taunted. "Admit it."

"What is there to admit?" I asked. "Honestly, I don't know what you see in her."

Lies.

I knew *exactly* what they saw.

Full, soft breasts that defied gravity.

A thick, supple ass and thighs that begged for me to spread them apart and take as much of her as I wanted.

A tiny waist that made me want to wrap my hands around it and crush her body against mine.

A greedy little mouth that could swallow my cock and, from the sounds of it, beg for more.

Her body was a temple dedicated to carnal sin, every inch of her skin begging to be worshipped. But her behavior grated on my nerves. She was arrogant and selfish, only caring about her own desires without consideration for others.

Callister regarded me with a gaze that saw too much.

"I know why you won't fuck her," he declared, his voice low and cautious. Suddenly he had everyone's attention, including mine. He took a long drag from his hookah, blowing smoke rings shaped like hearts before looking at me. "You're worried that if you give in to temptation, you'll lose control of your vampire nature and drink her dry."

Callister's words cut deep into my mind and stung whatever I had left of a soul. Every syllable of his declaration echoed like a dark prophecy. Although Callister and I occasionally had our differences, I suddenly hated him for revealing my greatest fear so effortlessly, and for all to hear.

My eyes burned with anger, yet I couldn't escape the truth of his words, no matter how hard I might try to deny it.

Would I fuck this woman if she wasn't my apprentice?

Absolutely.

But as long as I was her mentor, she was off limits.

She'd been summoned by my queen. Things were already dire in Wonderland. The last thing we needed was an Alice who had no desire to help us because she was sobbing her eyes out and nursing a broken heart. If this woman thought any of my friends were going to follow her home and live together happily ever after, she had another thing coming.

She was a plaything to them. Nothing more.

And I wasn't going to be part of that equation when she realized the truth.

"I have to give a report to Her Majesty," I said, rising to my feet. I didn't respond to Callister's accusation. There was no point. His mind was already made up whether I denied it or not. Instead, I finished the last of my wine and gave a courteous nod to Ransom. "Thank you for including me in your celebration. Wonderland is lucky to have you back at full strength."

Ransom, Hatter, and Chess all smiled and bid me goodnight.

Callister said nothing.

I didn't need to read his mind to know what he was thinking.

He was right.

My next lesson with Alice would only rekindle the fire of temptation. The thought both thrilled and terrified me, a dangerous game that I wasn't certain I could win.

"May the gods grant me strength," I whispered as I left the Great Hall, steeling myself for the challenges ahead. There was no arguing with the fact that this Alice was truly different from all the others. She was a test unlike any other, a battle of wills that would push me to my very limits . . .

And perhaps beyond.

I couldn't let that happen. I couldn't lose my grip. I had to remain vigilant. My duty to my queen outweighed any trivial matters such as emotions.

Feelings weren't part of my existence. Feelings belonged to creatures who didn't have to kill, to drink fresh blood to survive.

But Alice stirred something within me. Something . . . human.

And I hadn't been human in hundreds of years.

The only sensible course of action was to tamp down those intrusive thoughts. I was a knight. I had plenty of armor . . . physical and mental. I would use it all to guard my heart. For my sake, and for Alice's.

For Wonderland's.

As I navigated the secret path to my private chambers, I made a decision—a vow etched in the cold stone of my heart. I would do everything in my power to suppress these primal desires for Alice.

I would be her mentor, her protector . . .

But nothing more.

I knew that in the dance of predator and prey, the heart is the most vulnerable target, and I could not—would not—be the one to break hers.

EIGHT

ALICE

From dawn to dusk, I belonged to Jack, but from dusk to dawn, my time was my own.

Eight or nine hours of that time was spent sleeping. At least one hour was spent eating. One more for showering, brushing my teeth, dealing with my hair, and changing my clothes. Another hour was spent icing my newest bruises and sprains from the intense training until one of Amari's healing apprentices could fix me up.

It didn't leave a lot of time to play with my wicked boys or hang out with Queen Amari. She seemed to have her hands full and was constantly in meetings with bigwigs from her royal council.

There was a rumor going around court that the Red Queen's army was causing trouble near the border of the Kingdom of Diamonds and Ice, and the Kingdom of Hearts and Roses.

One night I tried asking Amari about it. She

simply said, "It's nothing to trouble you with, my dear. How's your training coming along? Jacques says you're making steady progress."

I don't know why, but knowing that Jack had praised me to the White Queen made me blush bright red.

"Yeah, he's a good teacher," I told her, then faked a yawn and went to bed early. I didn't mind hanging out in my Insta-worthy private suite.

The truth was that even with Jack's one-on-one tutoring, I was starting to feel the pressure of killing the Jabberwocky. The book Amari had lent me was simultaneously useful, and not helpful at all. I read every night until I fell asleep.

Apparently the demon had night vision that could put any Hollywood club's VIP room to shame, but bright lights were its kryptonite. It reminded me of trying to walk the red carpet in blinding flashes – totally disorienting. But getting a giant demon to walk past a horde of paparazzi?

Not gonna happen.

And even though this monster had decimated entire villages, it had a weak spot. Right at the base of its neck, the scales were way softer. Hitting it there was the secret to bringing down this nightmarish creature. It was like trying to spot the perfect Louboutins in a sample sale – not impossible, but good luck finding what you wanted.

"Ugh!!!" I groaned, and tossed the book to the end of my bed. "How am I supposed to get close enough to the Jabberwocky's weak spot in the first place? I'm not a demon slayer!"

A pair of brilliant green eyes appeared a few feet away from my face. They were floating in the air without a body.

I was completely unfazed.

"Hi Chess. How long have you been in here?"

"Not long," he purred. "I like to check on you from time to time . . . make sure you're safe . . . and not in need of anything."

"The only thing I really need right now is a foot rub."

I watched him materialize into his human form and sink down on the edge of my bed. He immediately reached for my left foot, kneading and rubbing it so well that I fell back against my pillow and sighed.

"Oh, don't fall asleep," he crooned. "I have plans for you."

The moment his lips curled into a sly grin, I knew he had something wild up his tuxedo sleeve.

I immediately shot him some serious side-eye.

"So help me, Chess . . . if the guys sent you here to ask me for a fivesome—"

"I've discovered a secret library," he hissed, his eyes gleaming even brighter with mischief.

I shot him a dubious look. "You're excited about a library?"

He shook his head. "No . . . a *secret* library."

"I still don't see the allure. Why's that exciting?"

"It's exciting because I've been visiting this castle for centuries, and never have I ever stumbled upon it . . . until now. I think it means something."

I snorted a laugh.

"Yeah, it means you're a nosy cat who likes to stick his nose where it doesn't belong."

Chess's grin twitched at my remark.

"Maybe I *am* nosy . . . but curiosity can't kill me. Shall we go explore it?"

"Why the hell not? It's not like I have anything better to do." I crawled out of bed and pulled on my Uggs and a warm, soft, cardigan coat.

Then I stopped.

"Why don't we invite the other guys? I don't want them to feel left out."

Chess's eyes lit up in wicked delight.

"Are you suggesting a fivesome after all?"

I couldn't help grinning at the hopeful undertones in his voice. My intense training regimen with Jack had initially been too exhausting for me to even think about sexy fun times.

But as my body grew stronger, my training with Jack was starting to feel less like swordplay and more like foreplay. I needed an outlet for all that pent-up sexual frustration.

And if Jack wasn't going to fuck me, I knew four other guys who'd jump at the chance.

"I'm just saying let's invite them," I replied with a flirtatious grin. "If you wanna snoop around and explore that place inside and out, it makes more sense to have all hands on deck. Don't you think?"

Chess's eyes sparkled with intrigue and desire as he led me towards the door.

"I think I couldn't agree more."

The wicked boys and I were now standing in a dark hallway deep in the basement levels of the castle. A thick wooden door reinforced with iron bars made it clear this place wasn't meant for the public's prying eyes.

"How did you discover this place?" asked Ransom.

"I'm a nosy cat who likes to stick his nose where it doesn't belong," Chess replied with a sly grin, then winked at me. "Can you think of something else you'd rather be doing?"

"Yes. I can . . . " Ransom mused, his dark, smoldering eyes leaving nothing up to interpretation. He'd been bedridden for days, away from the debauchery and sin of the Rabbit Hole. Even with the power of his Ring of Temptation, he still wasn't quite back to his full strength.

We all knew what he needed . . . what he craved. What he lived for.

Chess used his teleportation magic to slip effortlessly through the door. Moments later, we heard the clicking of an old lock turning before the door creaked open. We exchanged glances before entering, our senses tingling with anticipation.

Hatter cocked his head, his eyes twinkling with mischief. "Well, what are we waiting for? Let's investigate!"

As soon as I stepped inside, I felt the weight of Wonderland's history pressing down on me. The air was thick with dust and secrets, making it difficult to breathe. Even so, I couldn't help but marvel at the massive collection of scrolls and otherworldly artifacts that surrounded us.

Shelves upon shelves of ancient scrolls and leather-bound books towered into the gloom, their dusty spines holding untold secrets and forbidden knowledge. Strange artifacts glinted under the dim light filtering through high windows—a mummified hand, a mysterious bottle of glowing elixir, a skull etched with arcane symbols.

"Would you look at that," Hatter whispered, his voice barely audible as his gaze wandered over the rows of ancient books.

"Unbelievable," Callister murmured, running his hand over a strange artifact that looked like it belonged to another world. "I doubt anyone's been here in a hundred years."

As I explored the cavernous room, I couldn't help but run my fingers over the engraved titles, feeling the texture of the pages beneath my fingertips. My eyes drank in the arcane symbols that adorned them. The sheer amount of knowledge contained within these walls was staggering, and I felt both humbled and intrigued by it.

I glanced over at Ransom, who had picked up a thick, dusty book and was flipping through its pages with rapt attention. The King of Clubs was so tall . . . his presence was so commanding . . .

He was my demon daddy.

The ultimate symbol of masculinity.

I felt a rush of guilt as I realized I hadn't spent much time with him since we'd arrived here. I tried to catch his attention, but he seemed fascinated by the book in his hands. I wondered what secrets he was searching for – and whether he would find any answers in this old, forgotten library.

Suddenly his gaze flicked up and met mine. His dark eyes burned amber, then bright gold with lust.

"You and I have unfinished business, bunny," he murmured as he closed the book and set it down. Sensuality oozed from his pores, every inch of him inviting me closer and drawing me near. He reached out to caress my cheek, his touch sending warm shivers down my body. He'd been waiting so long for this moment. I could feel it in the air.

"Have you missed me, my king?" I asked, my voice low and seductive.

I could see the tension in his jaw as he nodded, unable to tear his eyes away from me, unwilling to hide his frustration. He grabbed my hand and pressed it against his crotch. I could feel his dick, rock hard and straining against his pants, yearning for release.

"You've been giving all your time and energy to

135

Jack," he growled possessively. "You should know better than to neglect your king in favor of a knight."

I smirked at him, relishing in the power I held over him. "Aww, is my king jealous over a guy I'm not even fucking?"

Ransom's eyes darkened as I teased him, a low growl resonating from his chest.

"Just for that . . . " he muttered darkly, and snapped his fingers. "No lube for you."

Suddenly my clothes evaporated into thin air. Ransom grabbed me and held me down on a wooden study table littered with ancient papers and scrolls. Leather cuffs curled around my wrists and ankles and bound them together, spreading my legs wide and putting my pussy on full display.

He snapped his fingers again, now standing before me in his full, naked demon form. A pair of beautiful black wings beat once, twice, then folded behind his back. Two sets of black horns loomed above me as he leaned forward and positioned his double cocks against each of my holes.

I gritted my teeth as he skewered me with his hot, thick length, then started pumping into me at a steady clip. The burning pain of the dry friction was almost unbearable, but knowing that I'd made him jealous had turned me on more than I'd expected.

"You want Jack to fuck your tight little cunt, don't you?" he growled as he slammed into me.

"No, I only want you, my king!" I gasped. Suddenly Chess was peering down at me from the other side of the table.

"That's not what you said the first night we were here," he taunted. "You told me you wanted me to breed you."

Ransom's eyes lit up in anger as he glared at me. "Hold on a minute—you were fucking the cat while I was fighting for my *life*?" He started fucking me harder.

"Well, someone had to fuck her," Chess reasoned with a polite shrug. "It may as well have been me."

"You sneaky little shit," Callister growled. "You told me she was already asleep, and not to bother knocking on her door!"

Hatter's mismatched eyes lit up with indignation. "You told me that she was busy fucking Callister, so I shouldn't interrupt them!"

Chess shot them both a dirty look.

"It was only fair, given that the moment I went to fetch the Vorpal Sword from the depths of Hell, you *all* chose to fuck her without me."

"Shut up, alright?" I shouted as Ransom continued to slam into my pussy and my ass. "I want all of you! I love all your different cocks!"

"Even mine?" Callister asked from where he stood, quietly observing.

My pussy clenched at the memory of his repulsive, insect-like, metamorphic dick. Just thinking about the way his dark teal shaft got narrower at the base and thick and fat in the middle made me ache to ride it again. I let out a groan as Ransom's harsh, dry fucking gave way to smooth, slick wetness.

"Callister," I moaned, even though it was Ransom

who was fucking me, "I love everything about your dick. Just thinking about it made me wet."

"Such a slut," he murmured in rare approval. "I'll let you have it once my friends have annihilated your cunt. Are you going to come anytime soon, Ransom? I think Hatter wants a shot at that ass."

I twisted on top of the table, feeling the sharp corner of a book digging into my back. I could see Hatter grinning like a madman, his tattered clothes and top hat still on, but he'd freed his cock and was vigorously stroking himself without an ounce of inhibition.

Ransom's thrusts became harder, faster, his hips slapping against my inner thighs. I could feel the strength in him growing with each stroke. I moaned his name, needing more.

"Take his cum," Callister growled from across the room. "You know you want it."

With a primal grunt, Ransom flooded both my pussy and ass with his hot, thick cum. I could feel both of his throbbing dicks pulsing deep within, filling every inch of me with his lustful release.

He let out a shudder as he slipped his wet muscles out of my holes. I groaned at the sad sensation of feeling so empty, especially when the hot cum started dripping from my pussy.

"Be a good girl and tighten up," Hatter scolded. "We definitely don't want to let a good thing go to waste."

He sidled up next to me and scooped me up, then sat on the edge of the table. I let out a deep, guttural moan as he slowly lowered my cum-filled ass onto his cock. I tensed up, tightening around him, but he had gravity on his side. He didn't stop until I was anchored against his balls.

Hatter's insane laughter filled the air as he withdrew from my ass just enough to slide back into it with one stroke. I gasped at the sudden intrusion, feeling him stretch me wider than ever before. He moved in and out slowly, his grin widening as Chess knelt down in front of me.

"Your scent is intoxicating," he purred, his tongue flicking out to taste my inner thigh. "And your cunt is still dripping with Ransom's seed."

To my sheer and utter surprise, Chess began to run his tongue up and down the length of my slit, teasing my clit, licking me, drinking me. While Hatter pumped in and out of my ass, Chess sucked my clit into his hot mouth, driving me wild with pleasure.

I threw my head back, resting it against Hatter's shoulder, wishing I could bury my hands into Chess's dark wavy hair. Every time I lifted my hips to his mouth, Hatter pulled me down deeper onto his cock.

Chess stood up, slowly and seductively peeling off his tuxedo. Then he leaned forward for a kiss. I arched my back involuntarily, moaning into his mouth as he teased it with his tongue. His warm saliva mixed with the musky scent of my arousal and Ransom's cum was almost too much. My clit throbbed and ached for release.

Chess fell to his knees again, this time exploring

my pussy with his magic demon tongue. My entire body tingled with anticipation as he alternated plunging into me with his tongue and sucking gently on my clit. He teased me mercilessly, drawing my orgasm closer to the surface in slow, sensual motions.

"Please . . . let me come!" I gasped, bucking against Hatter's strong arms.

"All aboard, Chess," he panted from behind. The Cheshire Cat was immediately on his feet.

"Are you ready for me, Alice?" he asked softly, tracing a finger along my collarbone. I craved his warm touch against my feverish skin.

One finger wasn't enough.

I needed *all* of him.

I'd barely nodded my head when he started cramming his thick, massive, girthy demon cock into me. His soft patch of bumps and nubs rubbed against my clit, gliding back and forth as we fell into a synchronized rhythm that threatened my very sanity. Their bodies felt like sin incarnate as they both claimed me at once, owning every inch of my being.

"You like being our little whore?" Ransom asked, stepping closer to watch me getting fucked by his friends.

I moaned in response, unable to form words as Hatter and Chess took me together, their hands roaming over my body, marking me as theirs. Each thrust brought unimaginable pleasure as their cocks stretched and filled me.

"You like being shared?" asked my king.

"Mmm hmm . . . " I whimpered.

As Chess and Hatter's movements grew more frantic, so did my need for release. Their hands gripped my thighs and hips tightly, guiding me through the motions as they ground against me, all of us desperate for satisfaction. The library fell away around us, replaced by the wet, slapping sounds of their fucking, our moans, and my gasps for air. Their skin gleamed in the torchlight.

And all the while, Callister looked on in silence. The only sound he made was to light a strawberry-scented cigarette.

"She's about to come," Ransom observed, stepping closer to watch. "Remind our bunny who she belongs to. I don't want her to even *think* about fucking the White Knight, do you understand?"

"Yes," Hatter and Chess replied in unison.

"Fuck her harder," Callister said in a sinister tone, breaking his silence. "Make her fucking *scream.*"

The room started to spin, the scent of strawberry smoke and sex filling the air like a thick fog. I felt powerless yet strangely empowered by their dominance, my body yearning for more.

I opened my mouth to cry out as my orgasm hit me and was greeted with the taste of Ransom's cum on Chess's tongue. My moans turned into uncontrollable sobs as I shattered on both of their cocks. My screams reverberated off the walls of the quiet library, each one louder and more desperate than the last.

My entire being convulsed with the intensity of my orgasm. Chess and Hatter's bodies continued to piston in and out of me in perfect harmony, prolonging my euphoria. I arched my back in ecstasy, lost in the delicious pleasure of our bodies melding together.

Hatter groaned, pulling me closer. His thrusts got harder, faster, his hips snapping hard against my ass cheeks. I could feel the strength in him growing with each stroke until finally he exploded inside me. My dark channel was filled with so much of his liquid heat that I wondered if he'd been saving himself for this moment.

Chess rode me harder, then let out a low, deep primal growl as his massive cock erupted inside of me, flooding my core with his scorching hot cum. I could feel every vein of his cock pulsing and throbbing as he released one load after another deep inside of me, drenching me completely.

As he took his pleasure and continued to pump every last drop into me, part of me couldn't help wondering if even in this moment, was he dreaming of breeding me? I shuddered at the thought as another warm splash of cum splashed my inner walls, soaking my cervix. I longed to wrap my arms and legs around him and hold him close . . . letting him enjoy the sensation of my body soaking him up, but my wrists were still attached to my ankles.

Chess's damp forehead fell against mine as he caught his breath. Green eyes glazed over for a moment, savoring the sensation of his cock nestled inside me. The old, familiar grin came back. Then he turned to Ransom. "Want another turn?"

Ransom shook his head and conjured a glass of wine instead.

"No, I'd rather watch Callister destroy what's left of her slutty cunt." He took a sip, then slowly walked over to the chair at the table and sat down behind me. "Don't hold back, my friend."

Callister stubbed out his cigarette and sauntered over to me with a wild look in his eyes and smoky strawberries lingering on his breath.

"Let's play a game, shall we?"

Still basking in the afterglow of an incredible orgasm, all I could do was nod my head.

"I'm going to remove your restraints. And you're going to pretend that getting fucked by the caterpillar is the last thing you want. Do you understand?"

He glared at me with so much intensity that I started to wonder if I should feel afraid.

"I want you to fight. I want you to scream. Don't let me down, Alice."

"Okay."

He waved his hands over my wrists, and the cuffs fell to the floor and crumbled into dust. Then he took out his deeply ridged, glistening cock. It throbbed and pulsed an unnatural shade of dark teal that faded to black. Somehow it looked both squishy and hard.

It was more revolting than I remembered.

And it was coming right for me.

"No!" I yelped, looking for the nearest path to escape.

But it was too late.

With a powerful, tattooed arm, Callister grabbed me roughly and slammed me face down onto the table. I squirmed against the papers and books, but he was so strong . . . so fucking strong. His hands were like railroad spikes nailing me down to the tabletop. My body tensed up as he lined up behind me. I felt the narrow tip of his insect cock push into my tightness, then felt the wide flare of the shaft stretch me painfully wide.

"Stop whining, you fucking whore," Callister murmured, his voice soothing despite the painful intrusion. "You can take it. You were built for this."

My fingers dug into the wooden table as I tried to adjust to his size. Every movement, every breath caused his cock to shift within me, stretching me out even more. The pain was searing but it was slowly giving way to a dull sort of pleasure.

I bucked and thrashed against him, but it was no use. When I looked up, there was Ransom, fully dressed and leaning back in his chair with a glass of wine . . . watching his friend plow me like we were just another show on Netflix.

"You're lucky he didn't go for your ass," he smirked, then took a leisurely sip of wine.

I let out a scream, genuinely worried that he'd only said that to suggest Callister ram his freakish, spiked dick into my asshole. I brought my knee

144

forward, then shot it backwards, hoping to push the worm off of me.

All it got me was a sinister, wicked laugh.

"Shhh . . . there's no use fighting it, you little slut," Callister's cynical voice was soothing and low, a stark contrast to the brutal dominance of his actions. His thrusts were slow but relentless and the alien shape of his dick made each thrust a new experience in sensations. To my relief, the spikes at the base were softer than they looked.

"Callister . . . please . . . " I managed to gasp out through gritted teeth, but whether it was a plea for mercy or encouragement, I didn't know.

He chuckled darkly, then repositioned me as he plunged deeper into me with every stroke. He was slamming into me with so much force that the table groaned under our weight. Inch by inch, it was slowly being pushed across the stone floor. Ransom scooted his chair backward, but kept watching in amusement.

Meanwhile, books and scrolls were vibrating off the desk and tumbling to the floor. I stretched my arms toward the edges of the desk, desperately grasping for something to hold onto.

My fingertips ran along a button of some kind that retracted when I touched it. A spring-loaded drawer shot out and smacked Ransom in the elbow, making him spill his wine all down his shirt.

"Fuck!" he snarled at me, but I didn't care.

"Is it true that you want Jack to fuck you?" Callister hissed as he kept pounding into me.

"No!" I whimpered. "I want *you* to fuck me!"

But Callister's accusation made the vision of Jack's gorgeous, yet cruel face drift into my mind. Long, straight hair of the palest blond tumbled down his broad shoulders. Intense red eyes . . . Sharp facial bone structure . . . a shredded, muscular body clad in black leather armor . . .

While Callister continued railing into me, I thought about the way Jack's abs could coil and curl as he fucked me. Callister had said the White Knight liked to play rough . . .

Maybe one day I'd find out.

Callister abruptly flipped me onto my back with a growl, inadvertently massaging my g-spot with the squishy deep ridges that ran along the length of his cock. The longer spikes near the base of it caressed the sides of my clit like a living, breathing rabbit vibrator.

With a fierce growl, he thrust deep inside me and held me in place, his muscles flexing as he tried to control himself. I could feel his cock swelling even bigger inside me, the pressure almost too much to bear.

Oh shit.

I remembered this from last time . . .

It was his knot.

I kicked and pushed at him, but it was too late. He'd swollen up so big and hard that I might actually rip my pussy in half if he pulled out now.

His knot stretched me to the brink of ecstasy and pain, and I knew I couldn't stop now. I thrust my hips against him, grinding against the squishy insect spikes

146

with desperation. With each thrust, the ridges swelled and rubbed harder against my inner walls.

So close . . .

Fuck—I was so close!

Every nerve in my body was alive with pleasure and anticipation. My fingers dug into Callister's tattooed arms, then clawed at his ass, trying to draw his disgusting, glorious cock deeper into me.

I pressed against him with all my strength, grinding against the spikes as if they were the source of all the pleasure in this world. My entire body was tense with anticipation, every nerve ending alive and begging for release.

More undulating from the cock ridges pushed me over the edge. I gasped for dear life and howled with abandon as warm, wet fluid gushed between our bodies.

"You filthy slut!" Callister shouted over my screams. "Did you just squirt all over me?"

"She got me, too," Hatter laughed from nearby.

I didn't even care. I was riding such a high that I didn't think I'd ever come back down. As one orgasmic wave after another washed over me, I lay back and let Callister fuck as hard as he wanted. As hard as he needed. The feeling of being filled by him, both physically and emotionally overwhelming, and I surrendered completely to all of it.

My drawn-out climax hit me so hard that I barely heard him moan in my ear. More warm, wet fluid spilled into me as he exploded inside my core. Even as the pressure of his knot subsided, he kept fucking with primal intensity, as if to make sure he'd completely drained his balls.

When he finally pulled out, I honestly wondered if I'd ever walk again. I glanced down and watched his sticky, purple, magical ball butter trickle down his shaft and his sack. More purple cum was dripping out of my gaping pussy and pooling on the desk under my ass, along with streaks of white from the other three.

Our bodies were slick with sweat, with cum, with my juice, and for a long moment, all I could do was lie there and catch my breath. When I could finally sit up, papers and scrolls were stuck to my lower back and shoulders.

"Alice," Ransom began, peeling a delicate sheet of paper off my sweaty ass. I noticed the wine spilled all down his shirt. Judging by the serious look on his face, I thought for sure that he was going to bitch at me for making him ruin it. Instead of holding a wine glass, he was holding a heart-shaped box. "This was in the drawer that you opened."

I blew a stray hair out of my face and gave him a quizzical look.

"Huh? What drawer?"

"The secret drawer you unlocked when Callister was fucking you. The one that popped open and made me spill my wine."

I blinked in confusion as my brain caught up with his words.

"That box was in the secret drawer?"

148

"Yes. And it's obvious why it's been locked away in a secret drawer . . . in a secret library. Look at it."

Still trying to catch my breath, I looked at him in disbelief.

"Can you give me a minute to clean myself up? I can't solve mysteries when I'm covered in cum."

Ransom rolled his eyes, but he was grinning.

"Go on, then. Clean yourself up. Let's see you put that imagination to work."

"Do I have to snap my fingers?"

"If it helps, then do it. The choice is yours."

I closed my eyes and tried to imagine myself not covered in sweat and cum from four different guys. I pictured myself clean, dry, and wearing my favorite cozies.

The sweat disappeared and my feet were suddenly warm, but something was off. I opened my eyes and saw that I was wearing my beloved Balenciaga sweatshirt and my Uggs . . .

And no pants.

"Nice try," Ransom snickered.

"Looks fine to me," Hatter hummed.

"You've nearly got it," Chess encouraged. "Give it another shot. Don't worry about snapping or closing your eyes. Just focus on exactly what you want."

I decided to put his advice to the test. There was a pair of Gucci drawstring track pants I'd been coveting on Net-a-Porter. I thought about the color, the stripes running down the legs, the cuffs around the ankles.

And then they were on me, wrapping me up in soft, cream-colored gorgeousness.

"That wasn't that hard!" I laughed in delight.

"It simply takes practice," Chess purred in satisfaction. "Now Ransom, what were you saying about the box you found in the drawer that Alice opened?"

"I think . . . I think this might be the Heart of Wonderland."

Ransom opened the heart-shaped box to reveal a broken fragment of a sparkling, glowing jewel. Its rosy red facets cast iridescent light in every direction, shimmering like it was a living, breathing thing. Even though I was dressed in my favorite cozies, my skin broke out in goosebumps as I found myself inexplicably drawn to the dazzling gem.

"Just look at it," he breathed, unable to tear his gaze away from the beautiful stone. "Can you feel the magic radiating from it?"

"Curiouser and Curiouser," Chess murmured in wonder. His green eyes reflected the red light emanating from the stone. The air around it crackled with electricity as tiny red beams reached out in an attempt to make contact with his skin. "It certainly *feels* like the Heart of Wonderland."

"Umm . . . guys? What's the Heart of Wonderland?"

Hatter stepped forward, his expression serious yet tinged with a hint of his usual whimsy. "The Heart of Wonderland," he began, his voice echoing slightly in the hushed room, "is more than just a jewel or an ancient relic. It's believed to be the very beating heart of Wonderland . . . a source of magic and power that predates even the oldest tales. It was born in the Kingdom of Hearts and Roses from the purest magic of Wonderland. It's rumored to amplify the true nature of whoever wields it, for better or for worse. Its power is immense, capable of shaping reality itself, bending the rules of nature and magic."

He paused, glancing at the fragment shimmering in the box as if they were long-lost lovers. "But as with all great power, it comes with a price—a balance that must be maintained. In the wrong hands, it would be catastrophic, but in the right ones, it could restore Wonderland to its former glory." His mismatched eyes met mine, filled with a mix of hope and warning, as if to underline the gravity of what lay in that little box.

"Dammit, Hatter . . . you ought to fuck more often," Ransom said, still holding the box in his hands. "That's the longest string of rational sentences I've heard you put together in years."

My heartbeat quickened, beating in time with the radiant pulse of the pinkish-red stone, and I felt an uncontrollable urge to touch it. I stretched out a finger towards it, feeling the same crackle of energy, but I pulled away at the last second.

Curiosity might not kill the Cheshire Cat, but it might just be the death of me.

"There's no way that little bit of rock is the Heart of Wonderland," Callister scoffed, but his eyes betrayed his curiosity as he leaned in closer. "The

Heart isn't even real . . . It's just a myth, a bedtime story for children."

"Well, it's definitely the heart of something . . . or someone." I pointed to the heart-shaped depression in the velvet lining of the box. "You can see where the jewel was broken. It looks like there's a bigger piece that's missing. See how this piece fits perfectly in the box?"

Chess crept closer, toying with his chin while his brow furrowed in thought.

"I can feel the power in this stone, but if this is truly a fragment of the Heart of Wonderland, why would Amari hide something like this from us?"

"Maybe she doesn't want us to know it's broken," I suggested. "Maybe she doesn't want anyone to know she has it. Or . . . " I took a deep breath as the next thought popped into my head. "Maybe she doesn't want anyone to know that she's lost most of it! Especially if it's so powerful that Wonderland would be totally fucked if the wrong person found it."

Callister let out a contemptuous laugh.

"I don't know how much more fucked Wonderland could become. It isn't exactly thriving right now."

"Well, it's not gonna hurt to ask her about it, is it?"

Callister raised a skeptical brow at me. "You want to tell Queen Amari that we broke into her secret library and went through her private possessions, then accuse her of destroying the Heart of Wonderland without any proof? I'll sit that one out."

I crossed my arms over my chest and frowned at him.

"Hey, if I'm putting my life at risk to slay the Jabberwocky, I think I deserve to know the truth about this magic rock."

"Maybe that's all it is . . . a rock." Callister lit a cigarette and was immediately surrounded by a swirl of cherry smoke. "If it was truly the Heart of Wonderland, she would've hidden it better."

"She did a pretty good job, locking it in a secret drawer in a secret library in the basement of her castle, don't you think?"

"Perhaps there's a way to test it?" said Chess. "Have any of you ever seen a stone with this particular color? It's not quite red, and it's not quite pink."

I sighed, knowing that if anyone in this room had seen the stone before, it wasn't me. I was the new girl.

Although . . .

There *was* something about that color . . . that shimmering, glittering pinkish red, that gnawed at my memory. I kept getting the feeling that I'd seen it before.

But *where?*

Tiffany's?

Cartier?

Bulgari?

Ransom closed the lid of the box and held his hand protectively over it. It was the same hand that wore a gold ring on his pinky finger . . . the Ring of Temptation.

Suddenly I knew *exactly* where I'd seen this stone before.

Only it wasn't one big chunk.

It was dozens of little pieces.

"The Red Queen's necklace!" I blurted out. "Ransom! When we tried to ambush her in your room, she was wearing a necklace full of rubies. I think it was made from the same stone!"

Chess's green eyes widened.

"You think Roxanne has the other half?"

"I don't know, but why else would she have refused to take off her fancy necklace if she was about to have sex?" I covered my mouth with my hands as my idea started to take shape and become a legitimate theory. "Dude! I've worn *tons* of expensive jewelry to red carpet events and awards shows. There's abso-lutely no way in hell I'd climb into bed with someone without taking off my fifty-thousand-dollar necklace first. Roxanne probably kept hers on because it's so powerful! Same goes for your ring! She wasn't wearing anything else!"

For a few awkward moments, the room was filled with complete silence. At first I wondered if I'd said the wrong thing.

But the more I thought about it, the more certain I felt that I was onto something.

"It is a possibility," Ransom said, eyeing the box with a bewildered expression. "But the necklace broke when you tried to cut off Roxanne's head. I recall beads flying everywhere before she flew into a rage. Between her soldiers and my staff, I'd be surprised if nobody's looted anything from my room."

"We could go back to the Rabbit Hole and look around," I offered. "All we'd need is one bead to compare to this stone. Then we can ask Amari for more details."

"You're not going anywhere," Ransom said with cool authority as he put the heart-shaped box back into the desk drawer. "For all we know, Roxanne could've taken over the club and left guards there to wait for my return. It's out of the question."

"I'll go," Chess volunteered. "I can teleport there and back before any of you get past the front gate."

Hatter let out a laugh. "No you can't! Not after that huge, monster load you just gave Alice! Your powers won't be restored for at least a few days. Maybe more."

If Chess had ears, I swear they would've flattened in irritation.

But Hatter was right.

The Cheshire Cat wasn't going anywhere.

"I'll go," Callister grumbled before tapping his ashes on the floor. "At least I can fight if I run into trouble."

"Nobody's going to the Rabbit Hole," Ransom said, his tone and expression severe. "We barely got out of there with our lives. It would be a fool's errand to send anyone else until we know what awaits us."

"Then what do we do?" I asked. "If I'm gonna have a chance of defeating Roxanne, it seems kind of important to know if her necklace is made of the most powerful magic in Wonderland."

Ransom nodded patiently.

"I couldn't agree more, but we have to be smart in how we go about our plan. We'll wait until Chess's powers have been fully restored. He's the only one who can teleport while remaining invisible. And Chess . . ."

The Cheshire Cat's expression perked up.

"Yes?"

"No more fucking until I say so."

CHAPTER

NINE

ALICE

The days blurred together like ink in water, each moment drifting into the next. I trained from dawn to dusk, showered, fueled my body like I was an Olympic athlete, then read my Jabberwocky book from Amari until I passed out in a bed that felt like it was made of clouds.

I pushed my body to its limits, running laps before my classes until my legs threatened to give out, then practicing drills nonstop. Jack and I carried out attacks and parries on the icy ground, on the balance beams, on crumbling piles of stones, on shifting sand . . . on whatever he felt like on that particular day.

Flashes of my old life in Los Angeles flickered through my mind less and less—red carpets, flashing cameras, adoring fans. How trivial it all seemed now. Here, in this stark, unforgiving land, I was so much more than an empty-headed socialite or a tabloid headline.

I was a warrior.

A champion.

Well . . . a champion in training.

But having a purpose in life gave me a reason to get up in the morning. I was starting to embrace the destiny that had been thrust upon me. The fact that my new personal trainer was hot as fuck didn't hurt, either.

When exhaustion clawed at my limbs, I pushed it aside. I had to. Wonderland's fate, and the fate of its people, rested on my ability to swing this damn sword.

One morning, less than an hour into our practice session, I landed a hit to Jack's ribs and immediately recovered into a defensive position. Unable to counterstrike, Jack stepped back and sheathed his sword.

"You're improving," he admitted, raising a mysterious eyebrow at me. "It's time you started wearing protection."

I looked up at him in confusion.

"Protection? From what?"

A fleeting whisper of a smile streaked across his gorgeous face.

"From *me*." He pressed his hand against the small of my back, leading me towards the weapons wall. "I'm going to stop holding back, and I don't want to risk hurting you."

Please, hurt me, I thought as an ache tore through my core. I'd spent countless hours feeling his powerful body pushing against mine, watching sparks fly every time our blades clashed, smelling his earthy, wintry scent, having him so close that I'd thought about licking the sweat off his chest. *Just shove me against the wall and fuck me already.*

Instead of shoving me against the wall, Jack held me in place and lifted my arms. My body trembled as his hands roamed mere millimeters over my curves. My breath quickened at the sublime torture of having Jack explore my arms and legs, my tits and ass, my inner thighs and my neck, all without laying a finger on me. His intense gaze studied me without explanation. Then his hands moved with deft precision, weaving intricate patterns in the air as he summoned armor from it, piece by piece.

A sleek, metallic collar hovered in the air momentarily before settling gently around my neck. "This," Jack explained, his voice a mixture of pride and concentration, "is the gorget. It protects your neck, a vital area, yet allows for full movement."

A larger silver shape materialized out of the air, and Jack buckled it around my torso. The metal was surprisingly light, almost like a second skin, yet I could sense its strength.

"The breastplate guards your heart and lungs. It's crucial, but it must not restrict your breathing. Is it too tight?" He stopped fussing with the buckle and looked at me intently. "You'll have to tell me if it's too tight."

"It feels . . . snug," I said with a shaky breath.

"Good," Jack murmured before slipping the strap into place. "That's exactly how it's supposed to feel."

Fuck . . . were we talking about armor, or something else? I couldn't help wondering if the innuendo I was picking up on was all in my head, or if Jack felt it too. I tried to push down the deep longing that he'd awakened, but the more he kept his distance, the more I wanted to shatter it.

And now he was touching me . . . using his strong, cool hands to prepare me . . . to protect me from the damage he might inflict on me. I wondered if he planned on giving me a chastity belt, because in that moment, I wanted him to destroy my pussy.

We stood together in front of the long mirror that ran across the room as he explained the function of each piece of armor, and how to put it on and take it off.

But I didn't remember most of it. All I could think about was the silky tone of his voice and the caress of his fingers as he fastened buckles up and down my arms, up my thighs, and up my calves, while saying words like pauldrons, vambraces, cuisses, and sabatons . . . .all in the faintest, hottest French accent.

"Now for your crown," he said, interrupting my salacious inner thoughts. He presented me with a masterpiece of craftsmanship that seemed to glow with its own inner light. "Your helm is your greatest defense, but remember—your greatest armor is your training, your wit, and your courage."

I took a moment to test out the feel of my new armor, marveling at how light and responsive it felt. Each piece was a stunning work of art, etched with patterns of snowflakes and embedded with crystals.

While I'd always thought of armor as something clunky and hard to get around in, this custom set seemed to anticipate my movements, offering protection without hindering my agility. Suddenly filled with a mix of gratitude and newfound confidence, I turned to Jack to thank him, and almost fainted.

My mentor was gone.

Standing in his place was a formidable presence, an embodiment of fear, respect, and wonder. Cloaked in shadows, Jack's red gaze pierced through the darkness of a devilish white horned helmet, a chilling reminder of his prowess in battle. His stance, both menacing and majestic, immediately scared the shit outta me, yet commanded my respect.

He was terrifying . . . and I was strangely turned on.

His armor was a masterpiece of craftsmanship, both sinister and sublime. It clung to his body like a second skin, its white metallic surface etched with scratches and dents that kept score of the battles he'd fought over the centuries . . . and won.

Even though it was made of metal, his armor appeared almost alive. The shoulders were adorned with spikes, reminding me of the jaws of the abyssal hounds, ready to strike at anyone who dared come close. The shadows kept shifting as if the armor was absorbing the light around him, giving the impression that this creature, this monster, this *thing* . . . was born from something darker than night.

Narrow slits in the helmet gave away none of Jack's thoughts or intentions, although just the sight of it made me want to run for my life. The two long horns that rose and curved above his head made him look more like a demon than a human. The only thing that reassured me that Jack was still in there somewhere was the shock of platinum hair that spilled out from between his horned helmet and his gorget.

He lifted the Vorpal Sword, then motioned for me to attack.

And because of the newfound confidence I had now that I was wearing armor, I lunged with such speed and precision that even I surprised myself.

The White Knight wasn't just going harder on me—that motherfucker was brutal. Relentless. That was the upside and the downside of having a mentor who demanded nothing but the best.

His grueling tactics pushed me to the brink of my physical and mental endurance, but as the hours and the days went on, he was slowly, methodically polishing me into an instrument of deadly precision. His burning red eyes held an unspoken promise—rise to his expectations . . .

Or crumble under the weight of failure.

I refused to crumble.

I'd been there, done that, and wasn't about to do it again.

If I fell down nine times, I got up ten. I practiced until my muscles screamed in protest, and honed my sword fighting skills under his unwavering scrutiny. Our movements had gone from an awkward series of

missteps to an erotic dance on the knife-edge of
death.

Jack pushed me to the brink again and again,
never satisfied until I was drenched in sweat and
trembling from exhaustion.

But with each punishing session, I grew stronger.
Sharper.
Faster.

Our swords clashed in a flurry of sparks and the
hard clangs of metal on metal. The air was thick with
the metallic scent of exertion and the icy sharpness of
the frost-covered walls that surrounded us. He
knocked the blade from my grip and shoved me
against the stone wall, pinning my wrists above my
head. I looked past his broad, spiked, armored
shoulder as my sword went skating across the icy
ground, far beyond my reach.

"Do you want me to go easy on you, little girl?"
he taunted, staring at me like a hungry white wolf.
The heat pooling between my legs betrayed how
much I craved his punishment.

"No," I breathed from the safety of my own helm.
I wanted him to ravage me, to break me, to mold me
into the weapon he wanted.

I lifted my chin and shot him a determined smirk.
"Do it again. And this time, do it harder."

His red eyes gleamed on the other side of his
horned helmet as his gaze raked over my body. He
started to let go of my wrists, then let out a growl.

My sword was suddenly back in my hand, just as

I'd imagined it. And the tip was pointed at Jack's chest.

"I didn't tell you to attack."

"I know," I said, openly gloating in satisfaction. "I was taught to take any shot my enemy is stupid enough to offer."

I couldn't see his mouth, but I could tell by the shape of Jack's eyes that a slow, wicked smile had spread across his lips.

"That's right," he said, releasing my wrists as he stepped away from my blade. He was definitely smiling. I could hear it in his voice.

Suddenly the cold edge of the Vorpal Sword was grazing along my throat. "Never let your guard down, Alice. Not even with me."

I woke up in the middle of the night to a dull, aching pain in my lower abdomen. I groaned into my pillow, immediately recognizing the familiar sensation of full-blown menstrual cramps.

But this was Wonderland. I tried to imagine my uterus not existing.

It didn't work.

I squeezed my eyes shut and concentrated harder.

Nope.

Still there.

I flipped onto my back and tried snapping my fingers to make it go away. That didn't work, either.

"Oh, come *on*! Uggghhhh!"

Apparently there were some things that even magic couldn't wish away.

Figures.

With a groan, I dragged myself from the soft warmth of my bed and rifled through the cabinets under the bathroom sink, quickly finding a box of tampons. Once I'd taken care of that whole situation, I conjured a peppermint mocha with extra whip, and washed down a couple of painkillers, steeling myself against the discomfort.

At least my use of magic was working well enough to create coffee on demand. Whenever I woke up from this strange dream, or acid trip, or whatever the hell this was, I was going to miss the magic of getting just about anything on demand.

I put on a fresh set of workout clothes and slipped on my Balenciaga sweatshirt and Uggs.

If I was wide awake, I might as well start my practice early.

The castle was still dark as I headed to the practice courtyard, but I could tell by the color of the sky that it was closer to dawn than midnight.

I couldn't help grinning at how early I was.

My tutor would be so proud of me.

My grin faded slightly when I stepped into our practice space and took in the latest version of my obstacle course. Judging by the contraptions hanging

from the ceiling, today was apparently rope
ladder day.

Gross. Hopefully my cramps would be gone by
then.

I walked over to the lowest balance beam and sat
down, feeling the chill of the icy ground seep through
my leggings. I'd forgotten the moment when every
muscle in my body had stopped aching and had
transformed into strong, toned symbols of all my hard
work.

I took another long drink of my coffee, such a
simple, small comfort, and shook my head at my
situation.

"Of all the bizarre twists my life could take," I
mused aloud, watching the steam curl lazily into the
air, "training to save a magical kingdom definitely
wasn't on my bucket list."

The intricate obstacle course loomed over me,
hundreds, if not thousands of knots hanging from the
ceiling. I wondered if the ropes had been
programmed to have a mind of their own. Would
they work to help me?

Not a chance.

That wasn't Jack's style.

Everything he did was intentionally designed to
make my life more difficult. When it came to the
White Knight, there was no easy button.

"Why am I even bothering with this?" I
wondered out loud before taking another sip of
coffee. The rich flavor of cocoa and the sharpness of
the peppermint offered a fleeting distraction from the

daunting reality that awaited me. "Am I for real right now? Chasing down a psycho queen and her pet demon with a magic sword? I can't even change a tire on my own car."

The absurdity of my situation would have been laughable if it weren't so terrifyingly real. Just weeks ago, my biggest concern was choosing the right outfit for a night out. It wasn't uncommon for me to change my clothes ten times before walking out my door. Now, the fate of an entire realm rested on my unsteady shoulders.

"I must be out of my mind," I continued, my voice a whisper lost among the whispers of the courtyard. "Or maybe I just like feeling like I actually matter to someone. To Chess and Ransom and Hatter. To Callister . . . Amari . . . to Jack."

The thought of Jack, with his piercing eyes and commanding presence, sent a shiver down my spine that had nothing to do with the cold. There was something about him, a mystery wrapped in an enigma, that drew me in despite my better judgment.

I traced the rim of my cup, contemplating the unknown depths of my new reality. The magical realm of Wonderland, with all its dark beauty and hidden dangers, was as enchanting as it was deadly. And here I was, a spoiled rich girl from L.A., thrust into the heart of its conflict.

I finished the last of my mocha, savoring the warmth as it spread through my body, offering a much-needed break from the cold. The sweet, chocolatey aroma mingled with the crisp air, a reminder of the small pleasures that life still offered, even in the midst of chaos.

I gazed at the weapons on the wall, their intricate details a testament to the brutality and magic of this land. They sat there undisturbed, but ready to defend Wonderland at a moment's notice.

"I'm doing this for all of them," I affirmed with newfound resolve. "For Chess and Ransom and Hatter. For Callister . . . Amari . . . and for Jack. For everyone they know who's suffering under the Red Queen's tyranny. And maybe we won't have to keep finding Alices to save this place. Maybe this time will be the last time."

With a deep breath, I stood up, feeling the weight of my decision anchor me. I was Alice Darling, former reality TV star, former failed lady boss, and I was fucking *done* with people who only wanted to see me fail.

Here, everyone was rooting for me to succeed. Here, everyone believed in me, even when I didn't believe in myself. They saw something in me that I hadn't realized was there to begin with.

Or maybe I'd just forgotten who I really was.

Hollywood had a way of doing that to people. Especially people who grew up around a camera crew and producers who coached you how to act in front of your own family. When everything surrounding you was fake, how could we know what was real?

The closeness I felt with Chess was real. My adoration for Ransom was real. My affection for

Hatter and my fascination with Callister were real. My desire to help Amari was real. My dedication to Jack was real.

If it wasn't, I wouldn't be in the courtyard.

The least I could do was give them everything I had.

I might've been the unlikely savior of Wonderland, but I would not back down.

I left my empty cup on the balance beam and walked over to the starting point of the obstacle course. There was training to be done, a psycho bitch queen to be defeated, and a destiny to be embraced.

And I was just getting started.

I did some stretches, then walked around the course, inspecting the ropes. I gave one of them a tug before daring to climb on and swing. I half-expected the rope to fall down and crush me or turn into a snake and bite me, but no . . . I just glided back and forth, swinging through the air like a kid at recess.

Nobody was there to watch me play.

No paparazzi, no reporters, no camera crew, no fans.

I felt so carefree. So relaxed.

It was lovely.

Out of the corner of my eye, the double doors to the room opened and Jack slipped through them like a shadow. I laughed at the bewildered expression on his face as he realized I'd beaten him to practice by over an hour.

Dragging my toe on the icy floor, I stopped swinging and jogged over to greet him.

My grin disappeared the second I saw Jack's expression.

His eyes were wide, and his nostrils were flaring. He looked like a wild animal that had been cornered. Then his expression hardened.

He took a step backwards, then another, putting more space between us.

"There will be no training today," he said abruptly. "You may go."

I blinked in confusion, then motioned towards the complex network of rope ladders. "Why? C'mon, Jack. I've already warmed up. I'm ready to go when you are."

He clenched his jaw, forcing himself to look away from me.

"We are *not* training today. Please leave."

His cold rejection hurt so bad it stung.

"Look, I know I fucked up on my first day, but I thought by now I've made it up to you. I thought you'd be thrilled that I've been here for over an hour. If you're not gonna train me today, I think I deserve an explanation."

Slowly . . . ever so slowly, Jack forced his head to turn in my direction. The way he was acting made it seem like it was causing him pain.

"You're bleeding," he said through tight lips, looking at me like I had a massive, gaping head wound that was drenching my face in blood. He took another step back.

I gaped at him, stunned and offended.

"So what? I feel fine."

Instead of answering right away, Jack stared determinedly at the selection of weapons mounted on the wall. He folded his arms across his chest, not bothering to hide his revulsion. "There will be no lessons until you're no longer bleeding."

"Why not? I'm perfectly capable of physical activity."

Pursing his lips, Jack shook his head, then took another two steps away from me.

"Dude, I'm just on my period. It's not like I'm dying of the plague and you're gonna catch it!"

Jack's jaw tightened and he winced like my words had punched him right in the gut. He looked like he was going to be sick.

"You should go. *Now.*"

Embarrassment and rage battled for my attention as I stared at him incredulously. Was this really happening?

"Very well. If you won't leave, then I will." Jack turned on his heel and stormed past me, his fists clenched at his sides. "Have Queen Amari send word once you're no longer bleeding."

My blood boiled at his blatant misogyny. Menstruation was a normal, healthy bodily function, not something unclean or shameful. His attitude was beyond infuriating and demeaning.

"Do you seriously expect me to just lay around doing nothing for the next four or five days?" I called after him. "We have work to do!"

My jaw fell open as Jack ignored me and slipped

out of the door, slamming it shut behind him. I stood
there in disbelief, shaking with anger.

I hated him.

I hated his fucking *guts*. What kind of shitbag
treated women like this? I was wearing a tampon *and*
clean underwear *and* clean yoga pants. It's not like I
was going to slide down the ropes and paint them
all red.

Fucking jackass . . .

That was his new name—Jack Ass.

The rope still hung from the ceiling, but the last
thing I wanted to do in that moment was to play and
swing on it.

All I wanted was to run back to my room, jump
into my bed, and cry.

Maybe I'd punch my pillow a few times.

But mostly I wanted to cry.

I slipped out of the same door Jack Ass had
slammed, and hurried back to my room before
anyone could see the tears in my eyes.

CHAPTER
TEN
ALICE

"Shit!" I hissed as I sat upright and threw back the covers. Golden yellow sunshine was steaming into my room. I was so fucking late for my lesson. It had to be well past lunchtime.

Suddenly I remembered that I had the day off. Maybe the next few days, for that matter.

Unless that bullshit from earlier had only been a dream . . .

I legit ran to the practice courtyard and burst through the doors, fully expecting to find Jack waiting for me with a disappointed frown on his beautiful, chiseled face.

The ropes and ladders of the new obstacle course were still set up like I remembered, but Jack wasn't anywhere to be found. Then I saw my empty coffee cup sitting on the balance beam. I remembered the way he'd treated me, and all my panic about being late for practice soured into low, seething anger.

I felt like such an idiot for being so proud of

showing up early to practice. I thought he'd be impressed with my dedication, and instead, he'd treated me like I was radioactive waste.

Why did he have to be so infuriating? And why, even now, did some part of me still hope not just to prove him wrong, but to win him over?

Maybe I was just hangry.

Food didn't fix everything, but it definitely wasn't going to hurt. I headed for the Great Hall to get some lunch. I loaded up a plate with waffles covered in butter and syrup and whipped cream and strawberries, added a side of fries, then grabbed a mimosa.

If I wasn't training, then I was going to eat whatever I felt like. I fully intended to bring my combo carb platter back to my room and eat in angry silence.

That plan went right out the window when I heard the familiar sound of Hatter's laughter. I looked up just as he, Callister, Ransom and Chess waved me over.

"What's wrong, bunny?" Ransom crooned. "You look ready to kill someone."

"Don't tempt me . . . "

Ransom glanced at Hatter, then over at me as I collapsed into the empty chair between him and Callister. "What's this? No training with the White Knight today?"

"Nope," I scowled. "Jack Ass is refusing to train me until further notice. Apparently he finds me repulsive in my current state."

The others exchanged confused glances, quickly followed by disbelief.

"But your current state is so lovely," Hatter reasoned.

Chess shook his head. "Jack would never—"

"He said what?" Ransom snarled.

"He called you repulsive?" Callister growled. The sneer on his tattooed face warmed my heart. If any of my wicked boys was going to go full-on vigilante mode to avenge my honor, it was the very grumpy caterpillar.

"Alice, what exactly did Jack say to you?" Chess patiently asked.

I crossed my arms, indignation burning in my cheeks.

"He said he won't train me because I'm on my period. He acted like I was diseased or something."

Understanding dawned on all their faces, although Hatter took a hot second longer than the others.

"He probably doesn't want to take any risks in harming you," he said, sounding strangely rational. "After all, his job is to keep you safe."

"Whatever. I thought his job was to turn me into a lethal weapon."

"Well . . . yes . . . but he already *is* a lethal weapon, my dear."

"A woman's monthly courses wouldn't be enough to set him off," Chess reasoned with a thoughtful smile. "It's not as if Jack is a young vampire in the grip of new bloodlust. He was a vampire for nearly a century before he came to Wonderland."

Ransom let out a sigh. "He's still a vampire. The

175

scent of blood has the potential to drive them into a frenzy."

"But Jack is well fed, and he's fought on countless battlefields and managed to keep his wits about him," Chess argued. "It would take a lot more blood than that to pull him into a frenzy."

I gulped my bottomless mimosa and listened while Chess, Ransom, and Hatter debated the quantity and the quality of blood and bodily tissue needed to trigger a vampire attack. The wicked boys were many things . . . but squeamish about female biology they were not.

Still fuming, I stabbed into my lunch with unnecessary force, alternating bites of syrupy sweet waffle with hot, salty fries.

Then a fourth voice caught my attention, whispering in my ear below the chatter.

"I know what Jack's problem is."

Callister's declaration was followed by the crackling of a cigarette being lit. A soft cloud of bright green smoke swirled out of his nostrils before curling above his head. Then he caught my gaze while a smug smile spread across his lips.

"Well? What's his problem?" I finally asked.

"Simple. He wants to fuck you."

I would've laughed in his face, if my mouth wasn't full. "I'm pretty sure that's the last thing he wants from me. You should've seen the way he looked at me this morning."

"You think I haven't noticed the way he looks at you?" Callister asked before taking another puff.

Apples. The smoke smelled like green apples. "Have you noticed any tension between you two during your lessons?"

"The only tension I've noticed is his obvious hatred of me," I said, shaking my head in firm denial. "He *loathes* training me. He's made that perfectly clear. In fact, he takes every opportunity he can to remind me how shitty I am with a sword."

Callister sat back in his chair, still grinning.

"Yeah . . . he might not enjoy training you, but he still wants to fuck you. Swordplay requires a lot of physical contact . . . a lot of trust in your partner. He was probably concerned that the scent of your blood would be enough to finally push him over the edge."

My angry chewing slowed down as I gave some consideration to Callister's insights. Maybe there was tension between me and Jack. Maybe it wasn't all in my head . . . especially if someone as cynical as Callister had noticed it.

Heat flooded my cheeks as I recalled Jack's abrupt dismissal and the revulsion in his body.

In his eyes.

What if he hadn't been disgusted by me at all? What if he wanted me so bad that it actually caused him physical pain?

What if it was more than simply struggling against his vampire instincts?

"Hey, Chess, how's your . . . um . . . *recovery* going?" I asked, ready to talk about something else. "Are you back to your old self yet?"

His permagrin faded, and Hatter let out a whoop of laughter.

"Oh, Alice . . . I think you've wrung every last drop of magic from the Cheshire Cat. It's going to be at least another day until he has the strength to visit you-know-where and look for you-know-what."

"It's not that bad," Chess argued with a surly frown. "I'm almost recovered."

Hatter leaned forward on his elbow, propping up his chin in his hand, giving me the most seductive smile I'd seen from him yet.

"Personally, I don't know what you find so alluring about a demon who goes limp for days on end, when you could have a fae who can keep it up as long as you can take it."

Chess's arm reached out and swiped across Hatter's face, knocking his top hat onto the floor. Hatter reached down for his hat, then retaliated by throwing the contents of a giant cup of tea in Chess's face.

The two of them fell to the floor and started to wrestle, but all Callister did was tap a bit of ash into a silver tray and roll his eyes.

"Care to place a wager on who comes out on top?" Ransom casually asked.

"Why not?" Callister replied confidently, his eyes sparkling with the thrill of the bet. "Five gold coins on Hatter."

Ransom raised an eyebrow, a playful smirk tugging at his lips. "Make it ten, and you're on. My money's on Chess. He's got that feline agility."

Callister snickered, shaking his head. "Hatter's unpredictable madness is his strength. He's like a storm – you never know where he's going to strike next."

"True, but Chess can read his opponents like an open book. He anticipates moves before they're even made," countered Ransom, watching the fight with greater interest.

Callister took a long drag of his cigarette, then leaned closer, his voice lowering conspiratorially. "Alright, let's up the ante. Twenty gold coins, and the winner gets Alice all to themselves tonight. His eyes immediately flicked over to me. "Unless you have other plans."

"I have zero plans until Jack Ass says otherwise."

I couldn't help grinning at him. I'd never had the Caterpillar all to myself, and I couldn't wonder if inside that hard, tattooed exoskeleton was a gooey, soft center.

"You've got yourself a deal," Ransom agreed, extending his hand to seal their wager. "May the best demon—or shifter—win."

As they shook hands, their attention returned to the ongoing scuffle, where Chess and Hatter were a blur of motion. Each move was as calculated as it was spontaneous. The air was thick with anticipation, the outcome of the fight anyone's guess.

Just as the wrestling match really got going, a streak of white shot past the corner of my eye. My heart did a somersault at the thought that it was Jack, coming to break up the playful fight, but it was another white-haired man. The one who'd led me into this strange, wicked Wonderland in the first place.

Winston, the White Rabbit.

His all-white attire was impeccable like I remembered, and his gold pocket watch dangled form his waistcoat. But his white hair was unkempt and his eyes were wild.

"Queen Amari," he panted, his voice filled with distress. "Have you seen her?"

"She's not here," Callister drawled, blowing smoke-rings absent-mindedly. "She's restocking her apothecary." He stopped watching his friends long enough to look up at Winston. "Do you want to place a wager on these two buffoons? They're just getting started."

Winston's face grew even more worried as his shoulders fell.

"I have no time for such games!" he said, wringing his hands together. "We have far greater problems than whatever they're fighting over. Amari . . . " he glanced around the Great Hall, twitching nervously. "I must find Amari."

"Easy there, Winston," Ransom cut in, his incubus charm doing little to calm the frantic White Rabbit. "What's got your whiskers in a twist?"

Winston's eyes darted around before he leaned down, his voice barely more than a whisper, as if sharing a dark secret. "The Red Queen has invaded a large village on the outskirts of the Kingdom of Hearts and Roses."

The nonchalant expression in Ransom's face disappeared, and he smacked Chess in the arm, prompting him to stop fighting with Hatter.

"Which village?"

"Echo's End." Winston took a deep breath before continuing. "We must inform Queen Amari immediately and plan a course of action."

I could feel the air in the Great Hall grow thick with tension. Most of the tables were empty, and most of the courtiers and servants were well out of earshot. But my friends exchanged wary glances, their previous lighthearted antics replaced by an all-consuming unease.

"Is there something particularly significant about Echo's End?" I asked quietly.

"It's very close to the border of the Kingdom of Diamonds and Ice," Ransom told me. His voice was calm, but I could hear notes of trepidation lingering beneath it. "With the sacking of this village, it means that the Red Queen is heading into Queen Amari's territory."

"War is coming," Winston whispered, his voice barely audible. "Whether Queen Amari is ready or not."

I felt a shiver of foreboding crawl down my spine as I took in the expressions on the faces of my wicked boys. Ransom's eyes were dark, his usual charm replaced by a grim determination. Hatter clutched the edge of the table, knuckles turning white, while Callister seemed to retreat into himself, his tattoos lifeless and colorless. Even Chess, who usually wore a smirk, had a grave look etched onto his face.

They all understood the gravity of the situation. Our laughter and mimosas seemed like distant memories, replaced by an all-consuming dread.

"Are you prepared, Alice?" Winston asked, his voice laced with a nervous hope. "Have the 'White Knight's teachings been enough to prepare you for the Red Queen and her Jabberwocky?"

The weight of his words hung heavy in the air, suffocating any remaining hope we might have clung to. My heart plummeted into my stomach, and I couldn't help but feel the crushing pressure of everyone's expectations bearing down on me.

As his expectant gaze met mine, my self-doubt reared its ugly head. Sure, I'd trained with Jack.

But was it enough?

The thought of facing the Red Queen and her terrifying pet filled me with a sense of dread and uselessness that clawed at my insides and made me want to throw up.

"Honestly, Winston," I admitted, swallowing back the anxiety that threatened to choke me, "I don't think I'm ready."

The silence that followed was deafening. I could see the disappointment and fear flicker across my friends' faces, and the ache of letting them down pierced my chest like a dagger.

The air around me seemed to grow colder, charged with a mix of fear and frustration and disbelief.

"Then we'll just have to make do with what we have," Ransom said, his voice a steely resolve that cut through the tension. "We've faced worse odds before, haven't we, Winston?"

"I don't think so," he replied, which only scared me more.

As we entered Amari's apothecary, the air was thick with the scent of herbs and magic. The White Queen stood amongst her apprentices, instructing them on which healing supplies to gather. She looked up as we entered the space, her eyes wide with concern. "Winston! You've finally returned! What news do you bring?"

"Your Majesty," he said with a polite bow. "We should speak in private."

Amari nodded, and her lips pressed into a thin line. She dismissed her apprentices with a wave of her hand, leaving us alone in the dimly lit room.

"Speak, Winston," she commanded, her voice steady despite the fear that flickered in her eyes. We arranged ourselves around a long table filled with bowls of different powders and strange looking plants. "Tell me everything."

"The Red Queen has invaded Echo's End," he began, his voice heavy with dread. "War is coming, and we're running out of time."

"Yes, we are . . ."

For being on the brink of war, Amari seemed oddly self-possessed. It probably had to do with the fact that this cycle had played out over and over again throughout her mysteriously long life.

"If her army is already in Echo's End, it will only take them a week or so to arrive . . . unless . . . "

"Yes?" Winston urged.

Amari picked up one of the bowls of dried flowers sitting on the table we were gathered around. She peered at the icy blue petals, smiling faintly.

"I can create a snowstorm like no other to swallow them up . . . blind them . . . and force them off course. It would buy us a few more days. Perhaps even another week, depending on how much frostbloom flowers my apprentices can locate."

"That's a brilliant idea!" Hatter agreed. "I can use my fae magic to grow as many frostblooms as you need."

"Chess, your ability to teleport will be invaluable in relaying information between our forces," Amari continued, her eyes bright with appreciation. "Ransom, I know you have connections in both Wonderland and Hell. Can you enlist any demon friends as allies?"

"Already planning on it, Your Majesty," Ransom replied with a sly grin. "I have quite a few old acquaintances who owe me favors. They're not fond of the Red Queen either."

"I can help create some ambushes," Callister suggested, stroking his chin thoughtfully. "Tree snipers, snow trenches, avalanche triggers . . . that sort of thing. If we can create enough choke points and ambushes, we can slow down their advance to a crawl."

"All of those are excellent ideas, Callister." Amari then turned to me. "Alice, as a newcomer to our world, you bring a fresh perspective. Do you have any ideas?"

I hesitated, feeling the weight of everyone's gazes upon me. Swallowing my nerves, I spoke up.

"Well . . . from what I know about the Red Queen, her biggest weakness is her short temper. If we can piss her off enough to make a stupid mistake, it might work to our advantage."

"Or it might get you killed," Ransom warned. "We'll handle the preparations for battle. You ought to focus on perfecting your use of the Vorpal Sword."

Silent humiliation spread across my neck and up my cheeks. I didn't dare tell any of them that I hadn't even held the Vorpal Sword since Jack had confiscated it upon our arrival. I started to panic.

"Speaking of which," Amari said. She trailed off for a moment to glance out the window. The sun was low in the sky, but it was still shining. She turned to me with a puzzled expression. "Why aren't you training with Jack right now? It's still daylight."

My cheeks flushed even darker, and my stomach was tying itself into more knots than the obstacle course waiting for me back in the courtyard.

"You'll have to ask Jack about that," Chess answered for me. "He canceled their session for today."

Amari's brow furrowed in concern, and she seemed lost in thought for a moment. Then she quickly adopted a confident face. "He's the Supreme Commander of my army. No doubt he's in emergency meetings with his scouts and briefing my soldiers. Don't worry, Alice. I'll speak with Jack. Time is running out, and he must finish your training."

As the strategy session continued, I listened intently while my internal conflict grew. The pressure to take action intensified, and I realized that time was running out for me to get ready. I couldn't afford to waste another precious second, but here I stood, doing Jack shit.

All because of Jack Ass.

Ransom's voice drew me back into the conversation as he outlined a potential ambush point. Hatter chimed in with suggestions for magical traps, while Callister offered insights on the terrain. Chess, ever observant, pointed out the locations most vulnerable to enemy infiltration.

The room was alive with the strategic planning breakout session. With each passing minute, the urgency of our situation became more apparent. I might've had an anxiety attack if not for the mimosas I'd chugged at lunch.

I felt like a fifth wheel standing there, listening to ideas that sounded way more fun than killing a demon.

Tree snipers?

Fuck yeah! Sign me up!

I couldn't shake the nagging feeling that I needed to do more. But it was made perfectly clear that I was only expected to show up and carry out the main event—slay the Jabberwocky. Defeat the Red Queen.

I still had so many questions about how to actually do the deed I was brought here for. I didn't even know if I was supposed to kill the Red Queen, or just the Jabberwocky. And I still had a bunch of questions about that chunk of ruby stone in the heart-shaped box in Amari's secret basement library. If the Heart of Wonderland had magic that would make things easier for me, I'd sure as hell like to know why Amari wasn't letting me use it.

It seemed like now was the perfect time to ask.

"Hey Amari, I was wondering something . . . "

My thoughts were tripping all over themselves in my head, and suddenly I heard Chess's voice beside me. He was invisible, standing with his lips right next to my ear.

I guess his powers were back.

"I know what you're going to ask her, and it is *not* the right time."

His voice was urgent, yet so soft that it sounded like a winter breeze blowing against the windows.

"Yes, Alice? What is it?"

I froze. Amari was waiting for an answer.

"Don't say a word, Alice," Chess warned under his breath. "Not a peep."

"Alice?" Queen Amari was staring at me expectantly.

Everyone was staring at me.

"I, um . . . well . . . I know you're really busy with planning a war and everything . . . " I choked out, stumbling over my words, "So you don't have to talk to Jack about my lessons. I'll talk to him myself."

"Well done . . . " Chess breathed into my ear. I felt a soft whoosh of air, and then suddenly he materialized behind the White Rabbit and the White Queen.

Amari blinked at me, then smiled.

"Wonderful. Yes, if you wouldn't mind speaking to Jack, I do have more pressing things to tend to."

Amari went back to her conversation with the others, while I contemplated what I'd just volunteered for.

The thought of confronting Jack made my heart thump a little harder . . . a little faster.

Maybe Chess was right, and Jack was merely concerned for my safety.

Maybe I was right, and Jack simply hated me.

Maybe Callister was right, and Jack just wanted to fuck me.

Whether it was one of the above, some of the above, or none of the above, I pushed the fear aside, knowing that it was time for the master and his apprentice to hash it out, once and for all.

ELEVEN

ALICE

I grabbed my practice sword from the weapons wall
of the courtyard and marched up to the first guard
I saw.

"Where's Jack's room?"

A pair of eyes slid down to look at me through the
armored mask, but the guard said nothing.

"C'mon! Don't you know who I am?" I scowled.
The irony of using that phrase wasn't lost on me—I
heard it all the time in L.A. but this time was
different.

"You're Alice."

I wasn't expecting the guard to answer.

"That's right," I went on, tossing my hair over my
shoulder as I gathered my thoughts. "So obviously
you know I'm supposed to save Wonderland, don't
you?"

"Yes."

"Okay, well I need you to tell me where Jack's
room is. He's supposed to be training me."

The guard shook his head.

"I can't tell you where the White Knight's chambers are."

So help me . . . this guard was twice my size, but I was about ready to bludgeon him with my practice sword.

"You can't tell me? Or you *won't* tell me?"

"Nobody knows where the White Knight's chambers are. Not even Her Majesty knows."

I rolled my eyes and started to walk away when the guard added, "The White Knight won't be in his chambers at this hour, anyway."

Suddenly he had my full attention. My scowl melted into a curious grin.

"Oh really? Where would he be?"

"Hunting."

I lifted a skeptical brow.

"Hunting? Like . . . out in the woods?"

The guard scoffed.

"Yes, out in the woods! It's forbidden for him to feed within the castle walls. Everyone knows that."

I decided not to inform him that special rules for where and when monsters were allowed to eat wasn't exactly common knowledge. At least, not for me.

Even so . . .

I had a brooding, Jack Ass vampire to find.

Leaving the castle through the giant front doors, I stood at the top of the steps and took a moment to admire the view. Twilight had given way to a starry sky splashed with the arctic palette of an intense aurora borealis. The snowy mountains surrounding the horizon were lit up in lime green, bright aqua, and brilliant purple.

A forest of pine trees topped in fresh snow stretched far and wide, interrupted only by jagged mountains of snow and ice. If Jack was hunting out in this wilderness, it would take me all night to find him.

I closed my eyes and conjured a thick parka, wool gloves, and tall, warm boots. I didn't know anything about tracking people or animals besides what I'd seen on reruns of Alone, but I knew that while Jack could jump far and high, he sure as hell couldn't fly. Maybe I'd be lucky enough to find some of his footprints.

I started walking around the perimeter of the castle, my eyes darting around, searching for anything that looked like a footprint. There was a shadow in the snow that led into the forest, and I headed in that direction.

Peering down at the tracks in front of me, I had no idea what had made them.

Was it from feet pushing through the snow?

Maybe it was from a small animal?

Or was it made by feet following a small animal?

Darkness swallowed me like sleep as I ventured deeper into the dense forest. My boots crunched in the snow, leaving a trail of prints behind me. The air was cold and crisp, scented with sharp pine and ozone-infused ice. Shadows flickered at the edge of my vision, stealthy shapes that vanished when I turned my head.

The feeling of being watched crept over my skin.

I shook it off, gripping my sword tighter, and quickened my pace.

Branches snapped and rustled around me, drawing closer with each step. The trail I'd been following had disappeared, leaving me stumbling between trees in the pale moonlight. Icy claws of panic closed around my chest, and I peered frantically into the darkness.

Something was *definitely* hunting me.

I prayed that the Red Queen hadn't sent assassins to kill me.

"Jack?" I called out into the frozen wilderness. "Is that you?"

An owl hooted softly in the distance. I rolled my eyes and blew out a relieved breath. Here I was, getting all worked up over nothing.

A single, small flash of pink darted across the snow in front of me, disappearing behind a tree. I froze in my tracks, my heart pounding in my chest.

Then my blood ran ice cold.

What I saw was a million times worse than assassins.

Fuzzy pink ears and a pair of dead eyes peeked out from behind the tree, staring right at me.

"Fuck."

Of all the monsters to run across in the woods at night, it had to be fuzzy pink bunnies. I cursed under my breath, gripping my sword until my knuckles turned white.

The bunny reemerged, hopping casually in my direction, its adorable twitching nose a perfect disguise for the vicious teeth within. My stomach twisted into knots as another fluffy pink ball of fur joined the first bunny.

Then there were four.

Then half a dozen.

More and more pink bunnies slipped from the shadows, surrounding me with deceptive cuteness. I raised my sword and whirled around just as they made their move.

They attacked as one—dozens of snapping little piranha jaws and razor sharp teeth. I swung my sword wildly, slicing through fur and flesh. I lost track of my kills after six or seven, not that it mattered.,

There were so many . . .

Too many.

Their teeth shredded my down parka to ribbons within seconds. Little white feathers were swirling through the air like it was a shaken snow globe. Pain exploded across my face as teeth slashed into my cheek. I grabbed the bunny by the throat, yanked it away from my face, and shook it until its neck was broken.

Another scream tore from my throat as a bunny latched onto my forearm. I felt a bunny leap onto my back, just as another one jumped on my leg. Thrashing and screaming and stabbing, I became lost in the frenzy of battle. I was going down, overwhelmed by a sea of pink.

A pale blur flashed through the chaos, and blood sprayed hot across my face. A tall, pale figure spun around the bunnies like a whirlwind, moving too fast for my eyes to follow.

Glints of silver flashed in the starlight. High-pitched squeals filled the air. One by one, small furry bodies landed in the snow, twitching and jerking on the ground.

Within a matter of seconds, the snow was strewn with blood-stained fur, decapitated bunny heads, and steaming entrails. The few bunnies left alive all fled into the darkness of the forest.

I sank to my knees, gulping lungfuls of air, and looked up at my blood-spattered savior.

Jack stood over me, chest heaving, eyes glowing deep crimson. His long, pale hair caught in the breeze, shimmering in the starlight. I might've mistaken him for an angel if it wasn't for the fine spray of blood covering his entire body . . . or his beautiful face.

Or the fangs bared to me.

He looked completely unhinged.

Feral.

My heart thudded against my ribs as I struggled to recognize the strange look in his eyes. I knew I should be afraid—terrified, even. But my snarly, brooding mentor had just come to my rescue.

The only thing I felt was a strange thrill of excitement.

"Run," he growled, clutching the hilt of his sword.

"Yeah . . . that's not gonna happen," I panted as I slowly pulled myself back onto my feet. My wounds were throbbing, and my torn, tattered clothes were covered in blood. "I'm not going *anywhere* alone when this forest is totally infested with killer bunnies . . . not to mention the Red Queen's army is already in Echo's End, wherever *that* is. For all I know, there might be assassins out there!"

Jack simply stared at me in disbelief.

"Run back to the castle *now* . . . " he ordered through clenched teeth, "otherwise I won't be responsible for what happens to you."

Oh, if this was the game he wanted to play, I wasn't having *any* of it. He could threaten and bully all he wanted, but I wasn't walking anywhere in this forest without using the buddy system. I wiped some of the blood away from the gash on my cheek and shot him a withering look.

"Hey, *you're* the one who walked out on our lesson today!" I snapped while pointing an accusatory finger in his raging, incredulous face. "You have one job—*one*—to teach me how to use a fucking sword! So why am *I* the one chasing you down for a lesson? What the fuck? And don't you *dare* try to hold me responsible for whatever happens to me when I'm not even *from* Wonderland! Not cool, dude! Not cool at *all*!"

A strangled sound wrenched its way out of Jack's throat, and the look in his eyes shifted towards maniacal.

Then dark.

Then savage.

"I warned you," he hissed, suddenly standing

over me. His left hand was wrapped around my throat before I realized he'd even moved . . . before the hairs on the back of my neck had time to stand up. The scent of copper swirled all around me, coming from the bunny blood all over his face, and the fresh bite dripping blood down my cheek.

Jack's eyes were wild. Possessed. "You should've run when you had the chance. It's taking every shred of strength for me not to kill you."

I stared into his glowing eyes and saw the raw, barely restrained hunger in them.

But I also saw something else: a flicker of recognition.

He *knew* me.

He'd saved my life.

I wasn't just another meal to him. Not even a snack.

I tilted my head to the side in defiance, my pulse racing.

"You won't kill me."

Jack ran his tongue over his sharp teeth and tightened his grip on my throat.

"Won't I?"

"No . . . " My voice was barely a whisper. "You need me more than I need you."

His eyes narrowed as they raked over me, and a flush of heat raced over my skin. My wounds stung as more blood trickled down my cheek, but the pain only seemed to intensify the heat building inside me.

"The only thing I need," Jack said, eerily calm, "is to tear into your soft, warm flesh. To drink deep of your blood. To fuck every hole of your entitled, overindulged body until you scream for it to stop."

A violent shiver ran through me. I hated how much his words affected me . . .

And how much I wanted him to make good on them.

I lifted my chin, refusing to cower.

"Do you promise?"

He blinked, seeming confused for a moment. Then a shudder went through him. A slow, predatory smile spread across his face.

He leaned down, his lips brushing my ear.

"I promise *nothing*."

Jack's grin widened, and he let go of my neck and grabbed a fist of hair at the back of my neck. I was expecting him to bend down to claim my mouth in a bruising kiss.

But no.

He struck with a snarl.

I never saw it coming.

Long, hard fangs sank deep into my neck. I cried out at the sharp pain while my hand instinctively flew up to push at his chest. But he only tightened his grip, pinning me in place against his body as he drank deep.

As he began to suck, an intoxicating warmth spread through my body like a champagne buzz . . . like my whole body was one giant clit he was sucking on. My struggles grew weaker, my limbs turning to jelly as he continued to feed.

Some distant part of me knew I should fight,

should push him away before he killed me. But his mouth on my neck felt so erotic, so exquisite.

It was like a new way of getting fucked, him pushing into my body, and me feeling the pressure, the pain, and then the pleasure. I moaned softly, tilting my head to give him better access to the holes he was buried in.

Jack made a low, hungry sound in his throat and pressed closer, grinding his hips against mine. I could feel his impressive dick, hard and insistent, even through our layers of clothes. The pain of his bite met with the ache in my core, awakening a different kind of hunger.

I moaned again, sagging against him as the pain throbbed throughout my body, mingling with pleasure. Two flavors at once, and I could taste them both equally. It hurt, yet it was delicious.

And somehow, in that frosty air that surrounded us, Jack was warm.

He was *never* warm.

But right now, with every mouthful of blood he swallowed, he felt like he had liquid fire running in his veins.

Cold metal pricked at my belly, sliding up my abdomen and between my tits. He stopped sucking on my neck just long enough to murmur, "Move, and I'll cut you."

I didn't know if it was a warning or a dare. I whimpered as the sharp edge of the Vorpal Sword pressed into my skin.

Still holding the back of my head with his left

hand, Jack lifted up his right arm, slicing away my sweatshirt and sports bra with ease. I shuddered at the cold air on my nipples. Arousal and fear twisted together inside me.

Then the blade slid down my hip . . . my thigh . . . and my calf . . . first the left leg, then the right. With expert precision, he sliced through my yoga pants. I trembled, torn between the desire to arch into his touch and the fear of injuring myself even more.

He brought the Vorpal Sword to my throat, pressing the tip into the bite he'd just left.

"Get on your knees."

I didn't need to be told twice. I fell onto the bloody, shredded remains of my coat and my clothes, sinking into the powdery snow. My hands immediately went for the silver buckle around Jack's hips, then tugged at the leather laces of his pants. I pulled out his warm, rigid cock and studied the pulsing veins that wrapped around the shaft.

Then I licked my lips and opened my mouth.

"Not yet, you greedy little whore," he said from above, pressing the tip of the sword deeper into the bite on my neck. I immediately sat back on my heels and looked up at him.

With his hand still grasping the hair at the nape of my neck, he turned my head to the side, leaving me confused.

Why didn't he want me to suck his dick?

I found out soon enough.

Hot, hard muscle pressed into the bleeding gash

199

on my cheek before gliding back and forth over it. I
could feel his dick smearing my blood all over the side
of my face.

Jack returned my head to face his cock, which
was now coated in bright red.

"You know what to do."

"Are you fucking seri—"

Before I could even finish my sentence, my
mouth was crammed full of bloody vampire cock. My
teeth caught on his delicate skin as he slammed into
the back of my throat. I choked and gasped for air,
but the more I struggled, the deeper the Vorpal
Sword cut into my neck.

I held as still as I could, grasping at Jack's
thrusting hips just to have something to hold onto.
Drool mixed with blood and ran down my chin,
down my neck, and yet, I found myself doing everything I could to suck the veiny cock that was invading
my mouth like a battering ram.

He swiftly pulled out and I was able to catch my
breath while he tormented my bleeding cheek with
the head of his cock.

"Again."

Before I could protest, he was already fucking my
face. My tongue couldn't keep up. I choked and
coughed, tasting my own blood. He pumped harder,
faster, then pulled out again. I started to turn my
head to the side, freely offering him my cheek, but he
pushed me to the ground instead.

Jack was on top of me in an instant, pinning me
down effortlessly. I squeezed my thighs together to

resist him, but he pried them apart easily in his powerful hands. He spread my knees wide, exposing my ass crack, my pussy, and my tampon string to the frigid wintery air.

His hungry eyes stared with growing arousal, and I felt a flush of intense humiliation creep up my neck. That burn of shame only got worse when he reached down and grabbed hold of my tampon string.

"Don't," I begged, barely able to look him in the eye. "Please."

He simply shook his head while a sinister grin spread across his face.

"You told me that you were perfectly capable of physical activity." To my horror, he started to pull on the string. "And what I'm going to do to you will be *extremely* physical."

He flung the tampon into the snow, then reached for the Vorpal Sword that lay nearby.

"*No!*" I screamed, landing a hard kick against his chest. "*NOOO!*"

Motherfucker didn't budge.

He didn't even flinch.

Instead, he ran his fingers up and down the blade until the edge of it was dripping with blood.

At least it was his blood and not my own.

A mix of horror and fascination held me captive as he reached down and slid his bleeding fingers into my tender, sensitive, bleeding pussy. I shuddered at the sensation of his wet warmth exploring my body.

"That's better," Jack murmured as he spread his fingers wider inside of me. He slipped them out and brought them under his nose. He took a deep breath, then sampled the taste of our combined blood.

Instead of licking his hand clean, he smeared the blood all over the head of his dick and his shaft. He stroked himself a few times before sinking his throbbing cock deep inside of me, tearing through my walls with a satisfied hiss.

I groaned in pain at the sudden intrusion, gasping for air. He filled me completely, stretching me almost past my limits. For a moment all I could feel was the pain of him inside me, hard and unyielding.

Then the White Knight began to ride.

Jack fucked me hard . . . without mercy, his hips pistoning as he drove that long, hard cock into my depths again and again. Every thrust punched the air from my lungs; all I could do was gasp and thrash and moan beneath his brutal onslaught.

The pain made room for the smallest bit of pleasure, sharp and sweet, as my pussy adjusted to his size. I dug my nails into the back of his jacket, clinging to him as he pounded against me. I could hear my own ragged breaths and the wet slapping sounds of his thrusting before it echoed into the silence of the forest.

His lips brushed along my throat, then found his bite from earlier. I whimpered as his fangs reentered the wound and latched onto my skin.

My blood spilled into his mouth in rhythm with his violent pounding. The dual sensations of him simultaneously drinking me and fucking me overwhelmed my senses.

I didn't belong to myself anymore.

I was his to use.

To fuck.

To kill.

I floated in a haze of ecstasy and pain, only distantly aware of the obscene wet sounds of our fucking. Jack was relentless. He ravaged me mercilessly, defiling my body without romance or restraint.

But I couldn't deny the pleasure that his savage passion was bringing out in me. He skewered into me with inhuman force, causing me to scream and writhe in pleasure and pain.

Each brutal thrust sent shockwaves through my body, driving me closer and closer to the edge of ecstasy, making me tremble and silently beg for more.

I had completely surrendered to his primal sucking and fucking, arching my back off the ground. I couldn't think straight. I couldn't breathe. I couldn't see. It was just a blur of white snow, red blood . . . a blur of pain, a blur of pleasure.

He railed me harder.

Faster.

Deeper.

I caught a glimpse of his cock and our surrounding skin covered in blood. I had no idea how much of it was mine, or how much was his, and I didn't care. All I wanted was to feel his throbbing cock inside me while I came on it.

Fuck, I was close.

I tilted my hips, angling my clit to rub against his body. His hands gripped my hips hard enough to bruise as he took me with an urgency that bordered on violence. The pleasure was bright and sharp, dancing along the edge of pain, and I relished every moment of it. His thrusts grew more erratic.

Suddenly Jack pinned my hips down. He held me still as he buried his cock to the hilt, shoving his balls against my ass.

Time stopped, and his eyes squeezed shut. A muffled groan vibrated against my neck as he took one last taste of my blood.

Then his balls twitched. He threw back his head and let out a wild cry as he fully erupted inside me, unleashing a torrent of liquid fire into my core. It felt like a scorching fire, filling me completely and leaving me gasping for breath. It was almost too much to bear, yet I found myself craving more, arching my hips to take him deeper.

His entire body shook and trembled, as if it couldn't contain the ferocity of his release. I could feel every twitch and spasm as he poured himself into me.

His cold, hard, impenetrable facade shattered as he surrendered to the ecstasy, consumed by the primal urges that had taken over his body. He didn't growl or roar like my other wicked boys.

No . . . Jack came so hard that his voice was reduced to a symphony of restrained moans and gasps. In that moment, he was no longer the most formidable swordsman in Wonderland. He wasn't the Supreme Commander of the White Queen's army. He wasn't even a deadly vampire.

He was a vulnerable man, lost in the over-whelming intensity of his orgasm, shuddering and gasping for air and trembling in my arms.

I savored the vision of his face, watching in slow motion as I brought the revered White Knight to his motherfucking knees.

In that moment, he was powerless, and we both knew it.

He rocked me with a powerful shudder and a few more thrusts, not so hard this time, just enough to finish draining his balls.

I'd done it.

I'd made that cruel, unaffected, holier-than-thou asshole lose all control. My body ached and burned, and I knew there would be bruises the next day.

But I couldn't stop smiling. I knew the bruises would be worth it when I saw the look on Jack's face.

His long, blood-streaked platinum hair fell to the side, revealing a foreign expression in his eyes.

Immediate regret.

Maybe even panic.

Still anchored inside me, still resting on his knees, Jack's red gaze wandered down the length of my body, then back up to my face.

"Mon Dieu . . . What have I done?"

It was the last thing I remembered before I fell into a void of darkness.

CHAPTER

TWELVE

JACK

I should've known better.

Now, my worst fear was coming true before my very eyes.

"Alice? Alice!"

My bloodlust had subsided, and a wave of remorse washed over me as I watched Alice's eyes roll into the back of her head. I'd taken too much of her blood.

Her breathing was shallow, her body weak from the savagery of our encounter. I knew I had to act quickly if I was to save her from the brink of death.

I slapped her across the face once, then twice, but it wasn't enough to stop her from drifting off. Her head merely flopped to the side, a faint grin lingering on her soft mouth.

Wherever Alice was headed, it was impossible for me to know.

Heaven?

Hell?

Somewhere in between?

And I'd sent her there.

After centuries of carefully managing my most primal desire . . . she'd borne the full brunt of my thirst, my hunger. In return, I had pushed her too far.

One look at her bruised and bloody body made me realize how grave of a mistake I'd just made.

I'd broken in plenty of Alices, but I'd never fucked one of them to death.

I pulled my cock out of her wet warmth and fastened my trousers, then lifted her into my arms.

Thanks to my heightened speed, nobody saw me enter the White Queen's castle. Nobody besides Her Majesty knew which chambers were mine and mine alone.

I debated whether or not to bring Alice to Queen Amari for a blood transfusion, then immediately talked myself out of it. The White Queen, my sovereign, my savior from the abyss of my own damnation, could never know of this betrayal.

For centuries, she had entrusted me with the sacred duty of training all of her Alices. She summoned them, these innocent young beacons of hope, to save our Wonderland from the clutches of her sister, the Red Queen. And I, in one moment of unbridled weakness, had not only fucked one, but possibly killed one.

The one that might matter the most.

The valiant knight in me, the one bound by honor and duty, was racked with guilt. I'd not only failed my queen, but I'd also failed this Alice . . . the very soul I was sworn to protect and prepare for the coming battle.

But the hunter in me, the one bound by insatiable thirst and the thrill of the hunt, of the chase, of the kill, was pleased by his conquest. I'd surrendered to my true nature, unable to resist the call of her flesh, the taste of her blood. She was simply too fresh and intoxicating.

My footsteps echoed softly against the cold stone floor as I carried the limp body of my young apprentice down to my silent, nearly pitch-black chambers. Situated deep in the bowels of the White Queen's ancient fortress, it was free from any chance of sunlight or prying eyes. The guards had long ago abandoned their patrols of this section of the castle.

Not even the voyeuristic Cheshire Cat knew how to find my lair, and that was saying something.

Knowing that Alice's treatment and recovery would be more effective if her body was warm, I brought her over to my bed and peeled off the bloody shreds of fabric that remained of her clothing.

A product of her imagination, the garments disappeared the moment they touched the floor. I quickly buried her under the covers, tucking the blankets underneath her blood-stained chin. My shoulders fell with a sigh as I considered how small she looked in comparison to the size of my large four-poster bed.

It was only then that my eyes widened in sober acknowledgment of what I'd truly done to this young woman.

As she lay unconscious and naked in my bed, I couldn't help but feel a mixture of guilt and lingering desire. The room was dimly lit by the flickering glow of a single torch, casting shadows that danced across her beautiful face.

She looked like a broken doll lying there, savaged by an unholy beast. Her skin was pale and her breathing was barely audible.

There was no time to waste.

I quickly conjured a hearty blaze in the fireplace, then went to the wooden cabinet where I kept my collection of potions and elixirs. My hands trembled slightly as I picked up a small vial filled with shimmering liquid—Timekeeper's Tonic.

A rare and potent brew, it was known among the best healers in Wonderland—healers like Queen Amari—for its ability to accelerate recovery from sickness or injury. It also gave the body the strength it needed to recover when time was of the essence. I always carried it with me to every battlefield I'd ever fought on here in Wonderland.

If anything was going to pull Alice back from the brink of death, it was this tonic.

As if I didn't already feel guilty enough for my sins of overindulgence, I had to sit with them until I'd brewed a pot of tea and steeped the tonic long enough. Heat was known to make the magic more potent.

Finally the teapot emitted a soft, luminescent glow, its shimmering contents shifting like the sands of time it was named after. I carefully poured the liquid into a delicate porcelain cup, then approached the broken creature who needed repairing.

"Alice . . ."

The moment I said her name out loud, I questioned who the voice belonged to. There was so much concern . . . so much *feeling*. Who was this man? The voice sounded so foreign to me that it took me a heartbeat and a half to recognize it was my own.

I sank onto the side of the bed and gently lifted my young apprentice's head, then brought the cup to her lips.

"Alice, I need you to drink this."

My voice was barely above a whisper, betraying a vulnerability seldom shown.

A vulnerability I'd forgotten myself capable of possessing.

A vulnerability I hadn't felt since I'd done the same thing with my dying wife and each of my children.

I needed this one to live.

My throat swelled up and my eyes stung and became glassy.

"Alice, please wake up. You were right. I need you more than you need me. And right now, I need you to live."

I felt so useless . . . so helpless. My hope was dwindling, and I could hear the desperation in my voice.

Perhaps that's why Alice fought so hard to open her eyes and see for herself if it was actually me who was speaking.

"Jack?"

Her voice was weak, barely above a whisper, but it sent relief through my body like a soft rumble of thunder. I hadn't realized how much I longed to hear the sound of her voice until I thought I might not hear it again.

"Shhh . . . don't speak. Just drink."

To my surprise, she parted her lips for me.

And it wasn't to shower me with insults.

As the Timekeeper's Tonic tea went down her throat, I watched Alice intently, hoping for some sign of improvement. The tonic seemed to flow down her throat and directly through her body, its magic working subtly, but working nonetheless. Slowly but surely, color began to return to her cheeks, and her breathing steadied. I watched it knit together the frayed edges of her vitality.

"Easy now," I cautioned, and took the cup away.

"Thirsty . . ."

"I know. There's no need to gulp. I made plenty of tea."

From the crook of my arm, she gave a faint nod, and I brought the cup back to her mouth. With every labored swallow, I watched over Alice with an intensity born from centuries of solitude and the weight of my actions. Unable to ignore every stray drop of tonic that dribbled down her blood-stained chin, I made a silent vow to do everything in my power to protect this fragile human.

She didn't know it yet, but she'd unwittingly become a part of my eternal existence.

A blood bond had been created the moment I pushed my bleeding fingers into her cunt, then fucked her with my blood-covered cock while I drank from her.

Was it unconventional?

Absolutely.

But it was still a blood exchange.

This knowledge both terrified and excited me.

As I held her in my arms and coaxed her to take more small sips of the Timekeeper's Tonic, my mind roamed to thoughts of her pinned beneath me, her hips twisting and begging me for more. Her cries of pleasure echoing in my mind.

I bit back a groan, unable to shake the images.

The guilt I felt for taking exactly what I wanted from her was tempered by the thrill of doing the same exact thing. Not only that, but the desire to have our bond grow even stronger.

I needed more of her.

But first she had to live.

Once the cup was emptied, I placed it on the bedside table and tucked the blanket closer around Alice, making sure she was warm enough.

I never minded the cold. In truth, I slept better when there was a bit of a chill in the air. But this Alice was from the land of sun-drenched beaches and palm trees. I lifted my hand and used my magic to coax another log onto the fire.

"What happened? Where are we?"

"We're in my chambers. You lost a lot of blood."

"Because of *you*," she murmured, as if realizing

for the first time what had transpired between us. Her eyes narrowed as she looked up at me, a mixture of anger and desire flickering within their depths. "You couldn't control yourself, could you?"

"Believe me, Alice," I replied, my voice tinged with regret, "I never intended for things to go so far. It was a lapse in judgment."

"Is that all it was?" she challenged, her gaze never leaving mine. "Just a lapse in judgment? Because it sure seemed like you were enjoying yourself."

'Enjoying myself' was an understatement. I'd craved her tender flesh from the moment I laid eyes on her. As much as I wanted to feel her heat again and again, I couldn't allow myself to give in to such base desires. Not when there was so much at stake.

"It was a lapse in judgment," I repeated, quickly regaining my composure. "One that won't be repeated."

She lifted a flirtatious brow.

"I wouldn't mind repeating it . . . as long as you don't kill me next time."

"There will not be a next time," I said, my tone sharp as a knife.

Alice shot me a disappointed frown.

"Don't you ever get tired of acting so self-right-eous? It's infuriating."

The thought of never experiencing the taste of her blood or the feel of her body against mine again was almost unbearable. Her taste was still on my tongue.

So sweet . . . so fucking sweet.

But I knew I had no choice. For the sake of my queen, my realm, and my honor—and for Alice's own safety—I *had* to find a way to resist her.

No matter how impossible it seemed.

"I won't apologize for holding myself to high standards. That's why this isn't going to happen again," I explained patiently. "We still have work to do. The fate of Wonderland depends on us. We cannot afford to let physical entanglements cloud our judgment."

The corner of Alice's mouth twitched playfully.

"I dunno . . . wrestling and sword fighting are pretty physical entanglements, don't you think?"

I narrowed my eyes at her, fighting to keep from grinning at her brazen reply.

"You know what I mean."

The flickering flames cast dancing shadows on the walls, on the bed, and on her face, creating a sensual ambiance that only served to remind me of the darkness we were both entangled in.

"Whatever," she scoffed before turning away from me. "I'll make sure not to cause another lapse in your judgment."

She shoved her face against the pillow and let out a groan, and I knew it was because of the bites on her neck and her cheek. The sound of her being in pain made my resolve waver.

"Alice, forgive me, but I still need to heal your wounds."

"Fine. Knock yourself out," she muttered, still staring at the medieval tapestry hanging on the wall.

It was one of very few relics that I'd kept from my

mortal life—a scene from my first successful hunt. I don't recall how long it took my mother and my sisters to embroider it, and I don't recall being nearly as appreciative of their gift as I should've been when they gave it to me.

By the time I was wise enough to understand how much time and effort they had invested in that tapestry, they were all long dead.

And I was immortal.

So it was not lost on me that Alice was now staring at an example of all the hard work and thoughtfulness that women so freely offered to arrogant men like me . . . and how much of it was never given much consideration, let alone a proper thank you.

This woman—this human from Earth—had gone to the trouble of fetching her sword and venturing out into the cold, dark woods in an unfamiliar land, all to hold up her end of a promise she made to save Wonderland.

An hour ago, none of that mattered to me.

All I did was attack her . . .

Fuck her . . .

Use her . . .

And now we were bonded, and she didn't even know it.

As much as Alice tried to hide it, I could sense her vulnerability and shame. Thanks to our newly forged blood bond, it was something I, too, felt deep inside.

I prepared a basin of warm water and a soft cloth,

then set about my task with a mixture of concern and restraint.

I dragged my thumb across one of my fangs, dabbing my blood on the bunny bite on her wrist, the one on the back of her hand, and another on her ear. Then I wiped them clean with the cloth, revealing perfectly intact skin.

I took her chin into my hand and gently turned her to face me. The blood bond had started to take hold. It was strong enough that I could sense that even though she was in pain, there was unresolved desire coursing through her.

I ignored it as best as I could.

The bunny bite on her cheek was deep, and dried blood was smeared all over that side of her face. I suddenly remembered the sensation of my cock pressed against that hot, wet gash, sliding in the slippery deliciousness of her blood.

Then I fell into the memory of Alice's lips wrapped around my length, taking me deep into her throat . . . sucking me . . .

Obeying me.

Was fucking her the only way to make her listen to me?

I could make that work.

No . . .

I wasn't thinking straight. I couldn't do something so depraved.

Or could I?

I'd already fucked her once, and she'd just more or less told me that she'd like to be fucked again.

A pang of longing cut into me like a blade, and my cock stirred below my belt.

Like my thirst for blood, it, too, was never satisfied.

It only got harder as I studied the most striking wound on Alice's body . . . the only one from me . . . the bite on her neck. Although it was a stark reminder of my loss of control, it was also a reminder of how exquisite she tasted.

Of how much I wanted her.

Of how I was willing to break my vow to Queen Amari and defile one of her precious Alices.

More than that, it was proof that I'd marked this one as my own.

When I hunted, I moved hard and fast . . . straight for the kill. When I drank blood, it was to the last deadly drop.

But when I tasted Alice's blood . . . I'd stopped in time.

I'd let her live.

I don't remember thinking about the reason why.

What if she was right, and I needed her more than she needed me? I'd said the words in a moment of desperation, before knowing that I actually *believed* them.

The realization hit me faster than lightning.

There was no 'what if' about it—she *was* right.

I could never let her know.

I bit into my thumb again and let my blood drip onto the gash on her cheek. Within a few seconds, the wound knitted itself back together beneath my

218

watchful gaze. Then I dipped the cloth into the warm water and washed away all evidence that I'd ever defiled her.

I sat back and rinsed the cloth in the basin, admiring the color of the water as it shifted from clear to red with Alice's blood. I wrung it out and cast her an expectant look.

"What about your legs?"

Having been surrounded by ladies of noble birth for most of my existence, I was expecting Alice to slip her ankles out from beneath the covers.

Such modesty was *not* in her repertoire.

Alice pulled back the blankets to reveal her entire body, including the blood-stained apex of her tender thighs. Then she slid a bare leg right into my lap. Her foot rested mere inches away from the hard bulge in my trousers.

"Yeah? What about my legs?" she mocked.

I closed my eyes and took a long, slow breath. My cock throbbed in response as I took in the scent of fresh blood from her cycle mixed with her scent of arousal.

My lids snapped open and I shot her a hard stare of disapproval.

She merely smirked, and I almost lost my composure right then and there. It would've been so easy to drag her into my lap and pull her down on my cock.

Yet she thought I was the infuriating one?

Ignoring the firelight dancing across the naked, bleeding female body in my bed, I focused on healing the various injuries scattered across her supple skin, my touch as gentle as I could muster.

"How come you're so warm?" she asked quietly. "Normally your hands are like ice."

"Drinking fresh blood does that to me," I replied through gritted teeth, focusing on a wound on her knee. I prayed that she wouldn't ask more questions. To my great fortune, she kept silent.

With every touch, I fought against the urge to indulge in her once more. Somehow, I managed to restrain myself, focusing solely on the task at hand.

As I finished tending to the last of her wounds, Alice's gaze met mine once again. This time, I caught a glimpse of something new in her eyes – perhaps it was a mixture of admiration and desire.

"Thanks for taking care of me," she whispered, her voice barely audible. "And for saving my life."

"Of course," I replied, trying to maintain my stoic demeanor.

"Those bunnies would've killed me if you hadn't shown up when you did. How did you find me so fast?"

"I could smell you."

Her eyes widened in concern.

"Do I smell bad?"

"No. Quite the contrary."

"What do I smell like?"

I couldn't help but chuckle. "It's not something that can be described in words."

"Will you at least try?"

"No. I won't."

As I dabbed the cloth against her knee one final time, she shivered, and a low moan escaped her lips.

"You know . . . this is only making me want you more."

My cock swelled even harder at the tone of her voice. But I would be strong.

I would resist.

I couldn't let her win this round.

"Jack." She pleaded, her voice thick with need. Her foot shifted in my lap, finding the proof that my cock wanted to be inside her more than anything in that moment.

"Control yourself, Alice," I warned, removing her leg from my lap as quickly as possible.

Had I given her the wrong tonic? She seemed almost fully restored, although I didn't recall this happening to people who'd taken Timekeeper's Tonic. "I told you—we're not doing that again."

"Why not?" She rolled onto her side, propping up her head with her hand, her eyes dark and seductive. "You've already fucked me once. What's *really* stopping you from doing it again?"

"I already told you—I lost control, and I won't let that happen again." My voice was firm, but inside I was battling my own desire.

"It's not fair," she said with a pout. "You got to come, and I didn't. That's really bad manners where I'm from. Not very chivalrous, either."

Her voice was a plea, a prayer. Loathe as I was to admit it, she had a point.

Damnable creature. Now she had me wanting to bend to her will.

But I wouldn't.

Not now.

I tossed the cloth into the basin and set it down on the floor.

"Don't make the mistake of assuming my title reflects my level of chivalry."

"Oh, I don't think that at all." I watched her fingers dance over her ribs, then curl around her breast until the nipple was a hard little protrusion. "The White Knight might be the most morally grey person I've ever met. I hope you get over your principles sooner than later."

I shook my head, although I was grinning in amusement.

"I won't."

Alice's eyes narrowed, a mixture of frustration and lust evident in her gaze. She huffed, clearly agitated by my refusal. Then she rolled onto her back.

"Fine. If you're not gonna make me come, I guess I'll just do it myself."

My pupils blew wide open and my grin evaporated. I thought I'd seen everything, but she proved me wrong when she slid her hand between her legs and parted her glistening folds with her fingers. I watched, transfixed, as she began to stroke the insides of her bloody thighs, her soft lips, and her clit.

"Stop it, Alice!" I snapped, clenching my fists. I turned away from her shameless, provocative display.

But my body betrayed me, my cock throbbing painfully against my trousers.

"Make me," she grinned as she continued pleasuring herself.

"Oh, you'd like that, wouldn't you?" I growled under my breath. I returned my gaze, unable to tear my eyes away from the twisted, debauched, erotic scene unfolding right under my nose.

"C'mon, Jack," she teased. "Gimme the D. I know you want to. I felt it with my foot. You're as hard as a rock, and I know you don't care that I'm bleeding right now."

Her eyes locked onto mine as she pinched and tugged at her nipples, her body writhing on my bed as she toyed with her cunt. But I couldn't give in. Not after nearly drinking her to death earlier.

"I think you wanna fuck me now more than ever. C'mon, Jack. You've already done it once."

Incensed, I leapt to my feet, jabbing an accusatory finger in her face.

"You're a spoiled little whore who's too used to getting her own way! Not this time, you won't. I will *not* fuck you again!"

"You don't have to fuck me." She closed her eyes, spread her knees wide apart, and slipped a finger into her pink, perfect, blood-tinged gash. "Just put in the tip."

I let out a twisted laugh.

"You think I don't know that game? Think again. I'm not playing that with you!"

Her breathing grew deeper and she let out one breathy sigh after another.

"Please, Jack . . . just fuck me one more time," Alice begged, her eyes pleading with me as she continued to pleasure herself. The room filled with the sound of her fingers massaging her slick wetness. The scent of her arousal hung heavy in the air, making it increasingly difficult to resist the urge to give in. "At least let me touch your dick."

"No."

"Okay, then you touch it. Let me see it one last time. Please . . ."

"Damn you, Alice," I muttered under my breath, unable to handle the torment any longer. But instead of stopping her, my own hand found its way to my raging erection and set it free.

She let out a low groan of satisfaction as she took in the sight of it bobbing and twitching above her.

"Are you sure you don't want to put in just the tip?"

"Shut up," I growled, but there was no anger behind my words – only raw lust.

Seeing my cock that close to her face was too much to bear, and I began stroking myself slowly, steadily, matching the rhythm of Alice's fingers on her clit and her glistening pussy.

Our eyes met, and for a moment we were lost in each other's gaze, our bodies wracked with frustration and desire as we pleasured ourselves. The tension between us grew more heated with each passing second, and I could feel Alice's climax approaching, just as mine threatened to overtake me.

"Jack . . . please," she wailed with pleading eyes. Her voice was broken and ragged with desire, making my cock pulse in my grip. "It hurts so much . . . I need you inside me when I come!"

In that instant, the last bit of my self-control shattered. The sight of her so wet and ready for me, supple legs parted and quivering, and her pussy glistening with blood-laced arousal was a vision that would haunt my dreams for centuries to come.

With a growl, I climbed on top of her, positioning myself at her entrance as her approaching climax made her body tense up.

"Fuck me, Jack!" she cried out as I plunged into her wet, welcoming heat. Her orgasm ripped through her, making her pussy clench around me, sending currents of pleasure coursing through my body.

Feeling her coming on my cock was like nothing I had ever experienced in all my existence – the perfect combination of tightness and warmth, her muscles hugging me, gripping me as if they never wanted to let go.

Her body enveloped me like a silken vise, pulling me deeper with each contraction, with every thrust. The blood bond we shared amplified our connection, making every sensation more intimate, every ragged gasp more precious.

"Harder," she demanded, and I immediately obliged, unwilling to refuse her anything. I groaned at the feel of her legs wrapping around me while her nails dug into my back, drawing blood.

Our bellies were slick with sweat, and I dove in deeper, thrusting harder.

"You wanted to come on my cock?" I grunted in between thrusts. "Do it again for me. You can scream as loud as you want, and nobody will hear you."

"No," she practically sobbed from beneath me. "Jack, I can't—I need—"

"Do it." I shifted the angle of her hips, grinding against her clit.

"Oh, fuck . . ."

I knew what that tone in her voice meant. It meant she was right back on the knife-edge of ecstasy.

Now to push her over it.

I pounded into Alice, driven by a fierce need to claim her, possess her, make her scream my name. Our coupling was rough and primal, all teeth and nails and pounding flesh.

My lips found hers, then pulled her in for a rough kiss.

She wailed into my mouth as her body seized, and an incoherent cry tore from her throat. I slowed down my fucking, watching her buck and thrash while her inner walls clamped down around my cock a second time.

Her orgasm tipped me over the edge. With a final, powerful thrust, I came with a shout. I unleashed a torrent of hot cum deep inside her, feeling my balls drain as I filled her to the brim. My cock throbbed as it pumped spurt after spurt of my seed into her greedy cunt.

And all the while, those long, supple legs held onto me, taking everything I gave her . . . and then some.

Keeping my cock inside her, I grabbed her waist and rolled onto my back so that she was straddling me.

Within seconds she was boneless and trembling, her limbs heavy with satisfaction.

Once she'd caught her breath, Alice lifted her head off my chest and pushed her long, sweaty hair out of her face, revealing a bewildered expression.

"How are you still this hard?"

I let out a low laugh.

"You wanted my cock . . . so you're getting it as long as you can stand it . . . " My tone suddenly became serious. "Under one condition."

"Okay, what is it?"

"Not a word of this to anyone. Especially Queen Amari. I can't have her knowing I've defiled one of her precious Alices."

The Alice perched on my cock let out a little snort, then giggled. I normally hated girlish giggles, but this one was . . . tolerable. Perhaps even a bit endearing.

Not that I would tell her.

"I hate to break it to you, but I was defiled waaaaay before I got here."

I raised a curious brow at her. "Is that so?"

"Yeah."

A strange sensation washed over me, perhaps triggered by her laughter.

I felt lighter.

Softer.

I felt . . . *playful.*

My everyday existence was spent with the weight of Wonderland resting on my shoulders. It didn't exactly allow me to escape reality and do something as sacrilegious as enjoy myself.

I could damn Alice to Hell or any other plane of existence. I could curse her name, but the truth was that I wanted to revel in the way it felt to be with her in this moment.

My fingertips traced an idle path along her neck, then her mouth, before caressing her golden mane.

"Then I take it you'll have no issue with me defiling you again?" I asked, grinning at her seductively. "After all, I've already fucked you twice. I'll fuck you all night, as long as you don't breathe a word to anyone."

"Not a word," she agreed. I watched as she sat up straighter, then began to gently roll her hips. I held still, letting her use me however she wanted. "I promise I won't tell a single soul."

THIRTEEN

ALICE

Studying my cheek and my neck in the long mirror that ran the length of the dimly lit practice courtyard, I couldn't believe how well my injuries from last night had healed. The deep gashes and bruises from the bunny bites and vampire bites were gone without a trace. Jack's blood was a magic salve . . . just a few drops and my skin looked good as new.

Better, actually. It was flawless.

I leaned closer and wrinkled my forehead, wondering if vampire blood could work the same as Botox. Maybe it was better.

If only I knew a guy for that . . .

I hummed in satisfaction, then leaned deeper into my warm-up stretches, savoring the delicious ache left over from Jack coming completely undone in my arms . . . .and coming in me and on me for most of the night. The events of the previous night played vividly in my mind, and I wasn't ready for it to end. I didn't want to let go of the memory of Jack's touch, his warm breath against my skin.

It was still an hour before dawn, and I hadn't gotten any sleep, but it didn't matter. I felt an exhilarating energy coursing through every fiber of my being. Every nerve ending in my body was awake and alive. The aftermath of our passionate encounter left me feeling alive and invigorated. There was no denying the intoxicating effect that Jack had on me.

I wanted him again.

And again.

"I thought I'd find you here." A silky yet serious voice broke through the silence of the courtyard. Startled, I glanced around but saw no one in the mirror's reflection. "Chess?" I called out with uncertainty.

Within a few seconds, he materialized a few feet away from me, dressed to the nines in a black tux with vivid green tiger stripes. The only thing missing from his ensemble was his characteristic grin.

"Where's Jack? Shouldn't he be training you?"

"He will, after he gets some breakfast," I replied, arching my arms over my head before bending to the left. "He doesn't want to train me on an empty stomach."

"Seems like he should've taken care of that by this hour . . . "

Chess still wasn't smiling. I pulled myself up to my feet and spun around to face him. He leaned in and with effortless feline grace, dipped down to breathe in the warmth radiating between my legs, beneath my breasts, and along my neck.

Then he shook his head in disapproval.

"Tsk, tsk, tsk . . . you fucked him, didn't you?"

"What? No!"

Chess shot me a rare, stern look. "Alice . . . don't lie to me. I know you didn't sleep in your own bed last night."

I folded my arms across my chest, trying my hardest to look innocent.

"Maybe I was with Ransom."

Chess grinned just a little bit wider.

"Well, that can't be true, because *I* was with Ransom last night."

Now it was my turn to be curiouser and curiouser.

"You mean like . . . you were *with* him? I know he goes both ways."

The Cheshire Cat demon stifled a laugh.

"Sorry if it's a disappointment, but the only hole we're interested in exploring is the Rabbit Hole. Since my powers are fully restored, I'm on my way there now."

My eyes widened. "Oh! Okay. I hope it goes well. Be careful."

"I'll be more careful if I'm not distracted."

"I'm not sure I know how to help you with that," I said, putting one hand on my hip. "We all know that every time I distract you, you lose your powers."

"That's not the type of distraction I was referring to." He tilted his head to one side, chewing on his bottom lip, silently deliberating on what he was about to say to me. "Tell me where you were last night, and then I'll know if I can trust you with what answers I get from the Rabbit Hole."

I glanced down at my sneakers, remembering Jack's specific instructions to me . . .

"Don't breathe a word to anyone."

"Chess . . . I swore I wouldn't tell a soul."

A glimmer of a grin tugged at the corner of his mouth. "Alice, I'm a demon. I don't have a soul. Technically, you'll have kept your promise if you tell me where you were."

I let out a long sigh, wondering when—not if—what I said next would bite me in the ass.

I did seem to be getting bitten a lot lately.

"Fine. I spent the night with Jack. I guess you smelled him all over me, huh?"

"Surprisingly, no. You washed away the evidence quite well. I just wanted to smell you," he purred, his gaze softening.

I furrowed my brow at him.

"Then how did you know I didn't sleep in my bed?"

He gave a nonchalant shrug. "I occasionally check in on you at night to make sure you're safe."

As endearing as it was, Chess and I were going to have to have a serious talk about boundaries. And just as I had that thought, he stepped closer to me . . . close enough to caress my cheek.

"*Are* you safe? Jack isn't exactly known for his tender heart. He didn't hurt you, did he?"

"Not too bad," I said, sugarcoating the truth. "I'd

232

let you see for yourself, but I don't want to jeopardize your mission."

"Fair enough," Chess nodded with a soulful gaze. "But you'll tell me if you ever feel it's going too far, won't you?"

"I will. I promise."

He gathered me into his arms, curling them protectively around my body, then nuzzled his cheek against my head. I could hear a low, deep rumble in his chest as he purred in satisfaction.

"I'm probably going to ask you about Jack every now and then, just to be sure. You said it yourself— I'm a nosy cat who likes to stick his nose where it doesn't belong."

"That's . . . that's really sweet of you," I whispered. My heart melted as I realized just how much he cared.

"If he hurts you, I won't be sweet. You've seen what I'm capable of. Jack might have fangs and the Vorpal Sword, but I have fangs and *ten* Vorpal Swords."

He stepped back and curled his fingers into claws, lightly dragging them down my shoulders and over my breasts. I threw my arms around him and kissed him on the cheek.

"Thank you, Chess. Thanks for . . . for being exactly the way you are, you nosy cat."

He gave me one last affectionate nuzzle before peeling himself away from me.

"I should go. There's somewhere else I have to stick my nose, unfortunately. But I shouldn't be too terribly long. I'll let you know as soon as I have news to share."

"Okay. Be careful!"

I lifted my hand to wave goodbye, but he'd already faded into nothingness.

Thirty minutes later, the Vorpal Sword glinted in my hands as Jack lunged at me, his own blade a flash of black and gold. I marveled at how light it felt compared to the cumbersome practice sword that I'd been using for weeks now. Jack and I were dressed in full armor, our bodies entwined in a sensual dance of clashing blades.

"You need to understand that the art of sword-play is as much about outthinking your opponent as it is about overpowering them," he said, blocking my swing and pushing me backwards. "You can't over-power me, Alice. You're certainly not going to over-power the Jabberwocky. But you can learn to outmaneuver it."

"Got it," I huffed, my frustration mounting with each failed attempt to land a blow. "Woman small. Jabberwocky big."

Our swords met midair, the impact jolting up my arms and rattling my thundering heart. I gritted my teeth against the force of his blow, holding fast.

"Your strokes are improving," said Jack, his voice

low and sultry. "But you're still holding back. You need to let go, but you're distracted."

"And whose fault is that?" I panted, circling my sword to meet his next thrust.

Jack smirked. "I believe you started this." He lunged again, and again our swords connected. I struggled against him, my arms trembling. "Last night I told you to run, and you didn't obey my orders."

"Do you fuck everyone who doesn't obey your orders, or just me?" I retorted, my breath heavy as I parried his thrusts. With every clash of our swords, I could feel the heat radiating between us. The intensity of the fight only fueled the ache growing between my legs, a primal desire begging to be sated.

Jack's red eyes gleamed down at me from inside his horned helmet. "Just you, Alice. Only you."

Fuuuuck.

The way he spoke those words made me want to surrender right then and there and pull him on top of me. Preferably while he was still wearing all the armor. With the helmet only revealing two black slits for his eyes, and devilish horns, he looked every bit like a monster who craved only flesh and blood.

I couldn't explain why, but I felt more connected to him now than ever before. I wanted his flesh inside me.

No . . .

I *needed* his flesh inside me.

With a twist of his wrist, he slid his blade along mine, bringing us chest to chest. I gasped at the feeling of his armor grinding against my body, his powerful thigh pushing between my armored legs. My clit throbbed for him. My body ached for him. And even though I'd fucked him all night, and even though I had a brand-new tampon in, I could feel my pussy getting wet and ready for him.

"Jack . . . I can't do this," I whimpered. "You're right—I'm too distracted."

"I'm not letting you get off that easily. Perhaps I should increase the stakes," Jack suggested with a wicked grin. He leaned in close, his lips brushing my ear. "You make me bleed, and I'll make you come."

A spike of heat ignited between my legs at his provocative words. "Deal."

With a renewed fire raging inside of me, I swallowed hard, summoning all of my strength and my imagination into the task at hand.

A growl rumbled in Jack's throat. He lunged forward, and I raised my sword to block him. Our blades slid along each other, and a shudder passed through me. I was acutely aware of the slickness between my legs and my nipples hardening beneath my armor.

I pushed myself harder than ever before. Sweat dripped down my body, soaking into the fabric that clung to my skin beneath the armor. My muscles ached, but I was determined to prove myself to my mentor.

As Jack pulled back for another attack, I imagined two very specific alterations in my breastplate— two perfect peek-a-boo holes that exposed my tits to the frosty air . . . and Jack's vampire eyes that missed nothing. He faltered for just a moment, his gaze snagging on my bare tits.

It was only a fraction of a second, but that was all I needed.

I lunged forward and swung with all my might. The Vorpal Sword sliced noiselessly through the air, and I felt the satisfying resistance as it connected with its target, sinking below Jack's left fauld and tasset and above his left cuisse . . . making contact somewhere below his waist and above his upper thigh.

Jack hissed before stumbling backwards, wincing as he reached into his armor with his free hand to assess the damage. Then he pulled his hand away and lifted it in front of his face. He tilted his head in disbelief, staring at the shiny red wetness. There weren't just a few drops of blood on his fingertips.

His entire hand was *covered* in bright red blood.

Even more blood was starting to spill down the shining silvery white armor on his left leg.

Holy fucking shit—

What did I just do?

His burning eyes fixed on me again, his red eyes glowing ferociously through the slits of his horned helmet, smoldering darker than ever before. My triumphant smirk immediately faded, replaced by a cold, sinking sense of terror and dread.

I cowered in fear of his retaliation, knowing I'd gone too far.

Jack stalked towards me, effortlessly knocking my

sword out of my hands. It fell with a musical, metallic clatter onto the icy ground.

In a flash, he'd closed the distance between us and slammed me against the stone wall of the court-yard. His body pinned me in place, one hand grip-ping my wrists above my head, the other working at the buckles of his armor.

My breaths came in shallow gasps as Jack only removed the armor around his hips. His furious eyes never left mine for a second.

"On your knees. Take a proper look at what you've done."

With my wrists still held above my head, I sank slowly to my knees, my heart pounding.

I gasped at what I saw in front of me.

A long, deep gash ran along nearly the entire length of his hip bone, bleeding such a steady stream of red that the crotch of his pants was completely soaked through. His cock strained against the fabric, rigid and thick.

He reached down with his bloody hand and freed his erection. It jutted thick and heavy between his thighs, flushed dark with arousal. Blood immediately streamed down his length, dripping down his balls, trickling over the veins before dripping off his swollen head.

"Were you trying to cut it off?" he snarled.

"No!" I gasped. "It was an accident! I swear!"

Still wearing the monstrous horned helmet, Jack shook his head.

"That was no accident. You saw a weakness . . . an opportunity . . . and you took it. Well done, Alice." His bloody hand caressed my cheek, then lifted my chin to demand I give him my undivided attention. "But you've made quite the mess. Clean it up."

A needy whine caught in my throat as I took in the sight of his cock. The shaft was slick with blood and precum. More blood kept trickling down, dripping on his leg armor, on the icy ground beneath my knees.

"Go on . . . clean it up." Jack's sword flashed, pressing against my neck as his other hand tightened around my wrists.

A thrill shot through me, warring with my terror. Jack wanted me to—

"Now," he hissed, nicking my skin with the edge of his blade.

I leaned forward and took his bloody cock into my mouth, letting my lips close around the swollen head.

The metallic taste of copper and iron and a touch of salt burst across my tongue as I sucked him deep, and Jack let out a guttural moan. He let go of my wrists and cradled the back of my helmet in his hand, setting the pace as I lavished my tongue over his length.

I took him deeper, doing my best to clean away the blood and precum. My pussy clenched over and over at the thrill and terror of being at his mercy.

Jack tore off my helmet and fisted a bloody hand

in my hair, fucking my mouth in sharp thrusts. "Just like that," he rasped. "Take it all."

His hips rocked forward, fucking my mouth in earnest now. The sword remained poised at my throat, a cold reminder of how easily he could end me.

I moaned around his length, cupping his wet balls as I swallowed him down again and again. I hollowed my cheeks and took him deeper, gagging around his girth. The sounds of my choking only seemed to spur the monster on, his thrusts becoming erratic.

His cock throbbed against my tongue. Suddenly with a snarl, he slammed into the back of my throat. Warmth flooded over my tongue and then he was spilling down my throat in hot spurts.

I struggled to swallow the mouthfuls of cum and blood, letting some of it spill from the corners of my mouth to drip onto my armor. I gulped down as much of him as I could, watching his wound start to heal, trembling as I waited for his reaction.

I yelped as Jack grabbed me by the shoulder piece of my armor and hauled me to my feet, then lifted his helmet enough to crash his lips against mine. Our kiss was bruising and deep, full of teeth and blood and lust. His tongue explored every inch of my mouth, sucking on my tongue, biting my bottom lip with his sharp fangs until I tasted my own blood. By the time he broke away, we were both panting.

"Well, this has to go," he murmured before removing the armor covering my hips and ass. One swift slice with his sword, and the yoga pants I was wearing underneath were now crotchless.

Still pressed against the wall, Jack lifted my ass and thighs like I weighed nothing, before draping my armored legs over the sharp ridges covering his shoulders.

"Watch yourself . . . I've been wanting to do this to you ever since I put the mirrors up."

I nodded my head and stared at the reflection of the inhuman horned creature who had me at his utter and complete mercy.

He leaned forward, growling in satisfaction as he spread me open with his mouth. When I looked down, all I saw was the devil looking back at me . . . the front of the helmet was like a second face watching me while Jack's real face was buried between my soaking pussy lips.

He tilted his head enough to stare at me while his tongue found my tampon string and twirled around it. I watched in both humiliation and desire as he caught it in his teeth, then squirmed in horror and fascination as he slowly pulled it out and let it fall to the floor.

All while keeping perfect eye contact.

I gasped at the sudden exposure, at the possessive gleam in Jack's eyes as he gazed upon my body, spread open and completely bared to him.

Then his tongue was back on my pussy, alternating between lapping at my folds in fat, broad strokes, and teasing my clit. He sucked the swollen nub between his lips, grazing it with a fang. I cried

out at the sharp pain, clutching onto him, only to melt
on his face the second his tongue returned to soothe
the hurt.

He licked his way lower, this time intentionally
letting his fangs pierce my outer pussy lips. Again, I
cried out at the pain, only to have him kiss it better. I
shuddered at the sight of his lips . . . his nose . . . his
chin . . . all covered in my blood and slick wetness.

How fucking depraved.

And how fucking perfect.

When he started sucking my clit again, I was
desperate to come, but I ached for the feel of his cock.
"I need you inside me," I begged.

"Not here," he replied, licking some of my blood
from the corner of his mouth with a faint grin.

"Then where?" I whispered.

In a maneuver too quick for me to wrap my head
around, Jack lowered me to the ground, then dragged
me across the icy floor by the back of the collar on my
armor until we were only a couple feet from the giant
mirror. He flipped me onto my hands and knees
before kneeling down between my thighs. The blunt
head of his cock was eagerly nudging my entrance.

"Do you want my mask on or off?"

My eyes flew open in surprise as I caught his gaze
in the mirror. His mouth was still covered in blood,
but now he was actually smiling.

Holy shit . . .

He was so fucking beautiful.

But the helmet . . .

It was fucking *terrifying*.

242

"Leave it on."

"As my lady wishes."

He pulled the front down into place, filling the vacant black slits with the crimson glow of his eyes. Then the horned monster behind me gripped my hips and drove into me, stretching my walls as he filled me inch by inch. I threw back my head with a cry, trembling around him.

"Keep watching us," he commanded. His eyes seemed to burn from within his horned helmet as he stared down at me, desire and something darker entwined in his gaze.

I vaguely nodded and met my own eyes in the mirror, seeing a wild creature staring back at me. Sweat trickled down my flushed face, and my hair clung to my damp neck. But it was Jack's reflection that truly captivated me – his demonic horned helmet made him look like something from a horror film.

At last he was buried to the hilt, his balls pressed against my clit. "So tight," he groaned, dragging back slowly only to slam home again.

I rocked back to meet his thrusts, clinging to the ragged edge of bliss. The metallic rattle of our armor clashing only turned me on more. His arm reached around my hip until his fingers slipped between my legs, circling my clit in time with his strokes.

The thrill of fucking a monster sent shivers down my spine, and I whimpered with need as Jack continued to drive into me, our reflections only amplifying the sensations.

"Come for me, Alice," the monster growled, watching me watching him in the mirror as he pounded into my depths. I arched my back, pressing my clit against his wet, bloody fingers, until I was unable to hold back any longer.

Pleasure coiled hot and tight as the first wave of my orgasm washed over me. The second wave was sharp and blinding, like a storm raging inside my body. I let out a scream only for Jack to clamp his hand over my mouth, muffling my cries.

He rode me harder, faster, pistoning as fast as my inner walls were squeezing all around him. His rhythm turned brutal, and he was pounding so hard into me that my face was mere inches from the mirrored wall.

At last he slammed deep and planted himself there, heat flooding my core as he came with a restrained hiss of pleasure. I felt Jack lean forward, the delicious weight of him making me collapse onto my forearms.

Together we fell to the ground, a tangle of limbs and harsh breaths. His cock pulsed and throbbed inside me, and I felt the liquid fire of his cum spilling over. We stayed there for a moment, recovering from the intensity of our encounter. Our breathing slowed, and Jack's grip on me loosened.

I blinked at the pale, pink clouds of nothingness that surrounded us.

"Jack? Where are we?"

"We're in the courtyard."

"No . . . " I said slowly, taking in my surroundings. "It looks like I'm sitting inside a giant pink cloud."

Strong hands pulled me backwards, and suddenly I was looking at my reflection—at our reflection. Jack was still anchored in my body.

"You're in the courtyard," he repeated. He caressed my bare ass and began gently thrusting into me again. "I pushed you through the looking glass."

"You mean there's been pink clouds on the other side since you put it up?" I asked, not sure if I was understanding correctly. "I could've walked through the mirror at any point?"

"Yes and no," he murmured, still fucking. I was so full of his cum that I could hear the wet, sloppy sounds of him plunging into me. "Yes, you could've walked through the looking glass at any point. No, there are not always pink clouds on the other side. I've never seen pink clouds when I've gone through it."

"Then what's usually on the other side?"

"Whatever you need there to be," he groaned, then tilted his hips to switch up the angle of his dick. "Sometimes I use it to visit my soldiers or different hunting lands. You probably saw pink clouds because your mind could think of nothing else in that moment."

I gasped.

Partially because his cock had just banged into my cervix, but partially because I couldn't believe my luck.

"You mean I could've been going to Starbucks

every morning instead of trying to magically make my
own pumpkin spice lattes this whole time?"

"Most likely, though I don't know what a star-
buck is."

"Come on over, and I'll show you."

The horned monster fucking me shook his head.
"I'm happy where I am."

I rolled my eyes, but I was grinning.

"Fine, keep fucking me. I just wanna see if I can
imagine a Starbucks on the other side."

With a handful of awkward movements, we
scooted our bodies over until we were parallel with
the mirror. Then we shifted to the left, sticking our
heads and half our bodies through the magic mirror
as easily as walking through a doorway.

Sure enough, I was in my favorite Malibu
Starbucks.

On the floor . . . on all fours.

Getting fucked from behind by a guy dressed like
a Satanic knight.

And it was *busy*.

I barely had enough time to see if my favorite
barista was working when a group of at least half a
dozen teenage girls tripped over us. A cold, wet bliz-
zard of pink and white filled the air as they spilled
their cotton candy frappuccinos all over the place.

Then they looked up at Jack . . . and started
screaming their goddamn lungs out.

My body lurched to the right, and suddenly we
were back in the icy courtyard of the Amari's castle.
Jack's dick was still buried in my pussy, but there was

a sound filling my ears that I didn't recognize. It wasn't the teenage girls shrieking.

This was a sound I'd never heard before.

It was musical in its vibrancy, full of depth as it echoed off the walls and lingered in the air. Strangely, my hips were vibrating in rhythm with the sound.

I twisted around to see Jack doubled over, his armor splattered with pink frappuccinos, and the front of his helmet pushed up to reveal his beautiful face.

His beautiful, laughing face.

Dear lord . . . he wasn't just laughing.

He was practically in tears.

"You want to do *that* every morning?" he howled, before erupting into another round of laughter.

The sound of his laughter was infectious, and the more I thought about those poor teenage girls trying to explain what they'd just seen, the more I started to laugh, too.

Still balls deep in my body, Jack gathered me close against his chest, burying his nose and blood-stained mouth along my neck.

"I guess you *do* know how to laugh, after all," I chuckled as I sank against his body.

"I thought I'd forgotten . . . but you make it easy," he mused. "I sorely underestimated you, yet you continually surprise me."

I tilted my head up, meeting his gaze in the mirror. "Admit it. You love it."

His lips quirked. "Perhaps I do."

And there amidst the depravity, the brutality, and

the blood shared between the two of us, I couldn't help but wonder if this was what it felt like to fall in love.

I adored all of my wicked boys in different ways, but Jack's cold, hard heart might've been the hardest one for me to break into.

The tender moment didn't last long.

Our little pink bubble of bliss vanished the second the courtyard door creaked open, and Amari stepped into view with Winston at her side. Their eyes widened as they took in the sight before them— Jack's cock buried balls deep inside me.

Even from the reflection of the looking glass in front of us, I could see the look on Queen Amari's face.

Her expression was as cold as the ice beneath my hands and knees.

CHAPTER

FOURTEEN

ALICE

"Jacques! What is the meaning of this?" Amari demanded as she marched up to me and Jack. Winston dutifully trailed behind her, his eyes wide with shock and disbelief.

I spun around in a panic, scrambling to magically repair the tear in the crotch of my yoga pants and cover myself up.

"Amari . . . I—" I stammered as Jack hastily pulled his cock out of me. "This . . . isn't what it looks like!"

Right at that moment, a massive wad of cum dribbled out of my pussy, soaking the crotch of my barely-mended yoga pants.

Meanwhile, Jack had calmly tucked his dick back into his blood-stained pants and risen to his feet.

"It's exactly what it looks like," he said without a shred of emotion in his cold, callous voice.

"How . . . how could you?" Amari's voice was

bitter, her expression one of complete devastation. "For centuries, you've served me loyally, and now I find you here, betraying me with my own apprentice?"

"With all due respect, Your Majesty, she's *my* apprentice," he coolly replied.

"I summoned her!" Amari shouted in his face, her gaze flitting between us. "I summon *all* of the Alices! They serve me just as you serve me! But it appears that you've taken your loyalty elsewhere!"

"My loyalty has been and always will be to you and to Wonderland," Jack insisted, his voice emotionless and firm despite the compromising situation he was in. "What happens between Alice and me doesn't change any of that."

Even though I knew his declaration was meant to sound honorable, it cut me like a knife. If Jack was that loyal to his queen and his kingdom, I'd always be in third or fourth place. Maybe lower than that. He was the Supreme Commander of the army . . . there were a lot of soldiers who probably outranked me as well.

"How can this level of involvement with Alice *not* affect your loyalty?" Amari challenged, and I had to admit, she had a point. "Did you have any idea that the Red Queen's army has invaded Echo's End? They'll be upon our doorstep within a week!"

Jack's face grew somber.

"Sorry! I was waiting for the right time to tell you," I squeaked, hoping to smooth things over.

It didn't have the effect I was hoping for. Jack stared at me like he wanted to give me a hand necklace instead of a pearl one.

"That's right . . . she knew *all* about the invasion," Amari said, looking at me like she couldn't decide if she was simply disgusted with me or truly hated me. "It almost makes me wonder if you *want* my sister to destroy our kingdom!"

Jack's crimson eyes flickered at me before pinning back onto his queen.

"It's never been an Alice's job to understand various military strategies," he said diplomatically. "Their only duty is to deliver the death blows to the Jabberwocky and restore peace to Wonderland."

"Haven't you ever wondered why peace never lasts?" asked a silky male voice that hovered above all of us. I looked up to see a pair of brilliant green eyes drifting through the air without a body to go with them.

"I have no time for your games, cat," snapped the queen. "Everyone knows it's because my sister is a monster!"

"Ah, but who made her that way?" Chess purred from above. His distraction was so effective that nobody noticed Ransom, Hatter, and Callister sidling up to Amari and Winston.

"What's going on?" Amari demanded.

"We could tell you . . . " Chess taunted as his body materialized, "but actions speak louder than words."

We all watched as he floated down to the cold floor. Ransom joined him, clutching something in his hands. I recognized it immediately.

The heart-shaped box.

Amari's eyes widened at the sight of it, her gaze flickering between the four men. "Where did you get that?"

"We found it in your secret library," Hatter said. "But I believe you already knew that."

"That box doesn't belong to you!" Amari hissed, her hands curling into fists.

Ransom shook his head. "It doesn't belong to *you*, either."

"What's in the box?" asked Jack. His hand was resting on the hilt of the blade sheathed at his hip, but I assumed it was only out of habit, rather than any risk of imminent danger.

"Oh, you'll love this . . . come have a look."

Ransom opened the box to reveal the glowing ruby-red stone fragment resting on a bed of red velvet. The light shone so brightly on Jack's face that his red eyes burned like crimson fire. Chess pulled his fist out of his pocket, revealing a collection of tiny red beads in the palm of his hand.

"Where did you find those?" Amari hissed. She started to come closer, but Hatter and Callister blocked her.

"Beneath a pile of dead bodies at the Rabbit Hole," He paused to give me a radiant Cheshire Cat grin. "Alice was right—they're from the Red Queen's necklace."

252

Then, to my sheer and utter surprise, the little stones vibrated and began to drift through the air, seeking out the stone in the box. It glowed brighter and brighter, lighting the way until the beads made contact and fused to the fragment in Ransom's protective hands. The rosy red light flashed so bright it was nearly blinding in its brilliance.

"It's the Heart of Wonderland," Ransom said with an air of deep reverence. "And it's the reason why the Red Queen has never stopped trying to destroy her sister."

"I . . . I don't understand," Jack confessed, unable to look away from the gleaming gem lying in the box. So many beads had fused to it that it was now over halfway restored.

"Not until you tell us the truth," Hatter said. "Why did you shatter the Heart of Wonderland?"

Amari's face paled, but her eyes blazed with fury. "I don't know what nonsense you're spouting. The Heart of Wonderland was destroyed centuries ago!"

"By *you*," Callister growled. "We know you smashed it to keep its power from your sister."

"What?" Jack asked in disbelief.

"Go on, Chess," Ransom urged. "Show them what the stone showed you."

Chess reached out and caressed the stone with a delicate finger, generating little red and pink sparks between his skin and the stone. Then, a hologram flickered to life up in the air around us.

"It's the stone's memory from when it was shattered," Chess explained.

253

"This is absurd! I insist that all of you stop this spectacle at once!" Amari demanded, her pious composure wavering.

Nobody moved.

"Jacques, as your queen I command you to put a stop to this!" she screeched. Jack looked at her, narrowed his eyes, then ignored her to watch the hologram tell its story.

We all stared, entranced by the scene unfolding over our heads as the memory flickered to life, casting an eerie red glow over the courtyard. As the hologram played out before us, it became painfully clear that Amari, the White Queen we all believed to be innocent and kind and compassionate, was not at all who she seemed.

We saw Amari and Roxanne as early teens, and watched Roxanne's natural magic abilities outshine those of her younger sister's. Amari grew more and more jealous of Roxanne, who was older, and always destined to be the rightful ruler of Wonderland.

In an attempt to become more powerful, Amari stole the Heart of Wonderland from the place it was born from—a hidden spring that flowed with the purest magic in the land. But when Amari's magic suddenly eclipsed her sister's, Roxanne quickly discovered the reason why. She confronted Amari while she was using the Heart, and demanded that it be given to her, since she was the rightful Queen of Wonderland *and* the more powerful magic user between them.

In a fit of rage, Amari smashed the stone and threw the pieces out her bedroom window, where they fell into a river and were carried away by the current. Roxanne ran to find them, vowing to reunite every last fragment of the Heart of Wonderland, not knowing that Amari had hidden the largest piece up her sleeve, keeping that magic for herself.

A heavy silence hung in the air as the hologram faded into the ether. The red light in the courtyard shifted back to its characteristic cool icy blue. I stood in the midst of my friends, realizing everything Amari had confided to me had been a twisted version of the truth. Jack, Ransom, Chess, Hatter, Callister, and Winston were all staring at her with a mix of anger, betrayal, and shock.

"Amari, how could you?" Winston asked, his voice shaking with a mix of anger and disbelief. "All this time, we thought Roxanne was the villain, but it was *you* who shattered the Heart of Wonderland."

Amari's eyes flashed with defiance as she squared her shoulders, every inch the regal queen. "I did what I had to do," she said coldly. "You have *no* idea what kind of darkness lurks within Roxanne. The power of the Heart would have only fueled her evil desires. I had to protect Wonderland from her."

"By destroying the very thing that held our world together?" Callister asked, a sardonic smile playing on his lips. "This is why we can't have nice things. Too many humans in Wonderland thinking they know what's best."

"Every decision I made was for the good of Wonderland," Amari insisted, desperation creeping into her tone. "I couldn't risk Roxanne getting her hands on the Heart."

"Even at the cost of countless lives—including my brother?" Callister asked, his eyes narrowed in disgust. "We could've been helping you restore the Heart of Wonderland and return it to its rightful place, but instead you chose to lie to us! You've doomed us all, Amari!"

"Enough!" Jack shouted, clenching his jaw in frustration. "Fighting amongst ourselves isn't going to fix anything. Regardless of what's happened in the past, we still have a common enemy. We need to work together if we're going to stop Roxanne."

"I'm not working with her," Callister snarled. "She's had centuries to do the right thing, and instead she's done nothing but feed us her lies."

"I made a mistake," Amari pleaded. "I was young and foolish and I made a mistake. All I want is to repair the Heart of Wonderland and make it whole again."

"And?" Callister pressed. "What were your plans after it was made whole again?"

Amari didn't offer an explanation, but Ransom had one.

"You were going to keep it for yourself, even though that level of magic was never meant to be used by humans. That's why you've kept it a secret all these years. You knew that Roxanne has spent centuries collecting the broken pieces, gaining more power and growing more corrupt every time she found another piece of the Heart. Meanwhile, your magic has become weaker."

He closed the heart-shaped box and slipped it into his pocket. "That's probably why you keep summoning more and more Alices . . . to use their innocence, their imaginations, their magic . . . because you've *never* had the strength to defeat your sister, have you?"

Amari's mouth was a tight, flat line. She didn't say a single word.

When Chess finally spoke up again, his voice was shaking.

"You willingly put little girls in harm's way to do your fighting for you? You hide behind the White Knight because you can't be bothered to risk your own life?"

"Amari . . . is this true?" Jack asked her, his voice heavy with disbelief.

They were just four little words, but somehow, some way, I just *knew* what Jack was feeling deep in his heart.

And it hurt.

The queen he'd faithfully served since his arrival had been lying to him for centuries. The lifetimes of unwavering faith in Amari had been deeply shaken.

"Amari . . . " he murmured again. "Is it true?"

Her lower lip trembled as a tear rolled down her cheek.

"I didn't know what else to do . . . " she whispered. "The balance of power between my sister and I has always shifted back and forth, but this time she's too strong. She's too powerful to stop, and she won't stop until we're all dead!"

My stomach roiled with anxiety as I realized what this was all boiling down to.

This sanctimonious nut job would've rather fed me to the wolves than admit she'd been a greedy little bitch when she was younger. All of this could've been avoided if she'd had the guts to ask her friends for help centuries ago.

But what bothered me the most was knowing that if the Red Queen and her Jabberwocky were sitting on her doorstep, she would've sent me out there to die.

It wasn't that Amari was evil . . . but she was definitely making some terrible choices.

I sure as hell couldn't trust her with my *life*.

My mind was racing as I glanced around the courtyard. My wicked boys were capable guys—they already had a plan in place to kill Roxanne and be done with the whole cycle of Amari summoning Alices. And after the White Queen's confession, I had a pretty strong feeling that this time would be the last time . . .

Whether I was involved or not.

The truth was that this wasn't my problem to solve.

I wondered if any of the guys cared about me enough to beg me to stay. I wasn't jealous of Amari—

she was a queen, after all—but man, I wished I had guys as devoted to me as the White Knight was to her. A pair of red eyes and a pair of green eyes swiveled in my direction as Jack and Chess picked up on my thoughts.

We had fun, but it's not like we're gonna live together happily ever after, I told them. I stood there for a few moments, waiting for a reply.

I got nothing.

Well, at least it was a more elegant breakup than when photos of Remy's side chick got leaked on the internet. Not every relationship had to end in a commitment.

"I think I'm done here," I said, casually stepping away from the group. "I appreciate the hospitality and everything, but I'm not really up for getting eaten by the Jabberwocky or killed by the Red Queen . . . or her army . . . or any fuzzy pink bunnies . . . or whatever else is out there."

"Alice . . . "

"Don't . . . "

"And Ransom's right," I added, still backing away. "Why would I want to fight for someone who hides behind little girls and White Knights? And now you want me to risk my life for you, too? It's just . . . it's just so gross. I can't even."

"Alice . . . please . . . "

I whirled around before I had time to change my mind. After all, self-preservation was human nature.

The looking glass running the length of the courtyard loomed before me, a shimmering portal that would take me back to the world I knew. Back to a life that seemed basic as fuck and relatively pointless compared to the insanity and vibrance of Wonderland.

With a deep breath, I lifted up my foot and stepped through to the other side.

FIFTEEN

I stumbled through the looking glass and landed back into the soothing, familiar surroundings of my favorite Malibu Starbucks. An immediate wave of relief washed over me at how easy it was to tap out.

Finally, I was back in control of my life. No more looming battles, no more arguing with irrational queens, and no more obligations to kill Jabberwockies. The warm, humid, ocean air and the scent of roasting coffee beans enveloped me, a comforting reminder of home.

But the scene playing out in front of me was *far* from comforting.

Tension hung thick in the air as everyone in the coffee shop was focused on a group of teenage girls . . . the same ones who'd tripped over me and Jack during our brief visit only moments ago.

They were huddled together, talking animatedly and using wild hand gestures as they gave information to a couple of police officers. One of the officers kept looking up from her notepad, her brow furrowing with disbelief, while the male officer took the report like it was just another day in Southern California.

Suddenly, one of the girls looked right at me and yelped.

"That's her!"

The high-pitched squawking that followed was instantaneous. I was so used to being recognized anytime I went out in public that I just rolled my eyes and headed straight for the door.

The male officer stopped me.

"Excuse me, miss. It seems there may have been an assault," he said, eyeing me suspiciously. "These young ladies claim they were attacked by someone who matches your description."

"Attacked?" I scoffed before shooting them a withering glare. "I didn't attack them! Those dumb-asses tripped over me!"

"No we didn't! You assaulted us!" one of the girls yelled.

"Yeah, you and that other freak you were with!" cried another girl.

"Jack?" I murmured under my breath. "Listen, we didn't attack or assault anyone. You tripped over us because you weren't watching where you were going."

"Our eyes work just fine! You jumped out and pushed us!" the first girl insisted.

"Look at my knee!" one of them wailed, pointing to a barely visible scrape. "I'm on the track team, and now you've torn my ACL and ruined my career! It's all your fault!"

"She should at least pay for lifetime Starbucks for all of us."

"Oh, I'm *definitely* suing her ass!"

"Yeah! That crazy bitch came out of fucking nowhere and jumped in front of us!"

"No, we didn't! I argued. I was starting to lose my patience with these morons. "We poked our heads through the looking glass and you tripped on us!"

"Looking glass?" the male officer raised an eyebrow, clicking the end of his pen as he studied my face. "When you say looking glass, what exactly do you mean?"

I hooked my thumb over my shoulder. "I'm talking about the giant mirror behind me that leads to Wonderland. Duh."

The most vocal of the girls, probably the leader of the she-wolf pack, folded her arms and gave me a holier-than-though look.

"Wonderland? Okay, bestie," she mocked, her voice dripping with sarcasm. "Tell the nice officers all about the giant mirror behind you that leads to another world."

I narrowed my eyes, shooting daggers at her. Those metaphorical daggers might as well have hit a metaphorical forcefield shield surrounding her, because they weren't getting through.

High school girls were the worst. I knew because I'd been one.

"I *will* tell them, bitch. Watch me."

I spun on my heel and started walking back between the two tables from where I'd emerged, expecting to find myself in the icy courtyard where Jack and Amari were probably still arguing.

Nothing happened.

All I saw were the giant picture windows that lined the Starbucks building, and the wonky little trees that grew between the glass and the parking lot.

I walked back and forth, frowning in confusion. Finally, I walked around the tables and chairs. Then I reached out into the open air, taking slow, cautious steps until my fingers pawed at the windows.

Still, nothing happened.

"It was right here a second ago . . . " I muttered, genuinely mystified.

Then the whispers started, creating a ripple of excitement coursing through the Starbucks patrons. A few of the girls started laughing.

"What a psycho!"

"Oh my god! Is that—is that who I think it is?"

"Alice Darling? Holy shit—you're right!"

"She's obviously on drugs," another girl chimed in with a sense of authority. "Look at her. Did you see that video on YouTube of her falling out of a limo without any underwear on?"

"Yeah! Did you hear that she hired a bunch of child laborers to make her shoes in some horrendous overseas sweatshop?"

"What a greedy piece of shit," the ringleader said before casting her judgmental gaze at me. "Hey Alice! Do *better!*"

My heart was thumping so fast that I felt like throwing up. I needed to get out of there before these underage bitches ate me alive or the paparazzi showed up.

"Officer, I swear I didn't do anything wrong. It's all just a misunderstanding. Please, I just need to get home. My lawyers can deal with whatever questions you have."

Alice? My heart froze at the sound of Jack's voice in my head. *Where are you?*

"I'm at Starbucks. Can you get me out of here?"

I'm trying find you, but I don't remember what it looked like. I was only there for five seconds.

"It's got big windows," I told him, whirling around as I tried to find him.

"Who the fuck is she talking to?" one of the girls asked her friend.

The two police officers shared a glance. Then one of them called for backup. I knew the codes for murder and robbery and an overdose, but I didn't recognize the code they called in for me.

Desperation clawed at my throat. Why was no one listening to me? Why did no one believe me?

I rubbed my temple and gazed down at my feet . . . my silvery-gold encased feet, and that's when it dawned on me—

I was still dressed in my battle armor.

I lifted my left arm in front of my face, studying

265

the intricate engravings on the custom-built gauntlets Jack had created for me. Anxiety bloomed throughout my entire body as I looked at my armor, then at the Starbucks seasonal menu, then back to my armor.

"This isn't what it looks like," I said, my voice shaking. "I'm perfectly sane."

"I dunno, it kinda looks like Alice Darling is having a mental health crisis at Starbucks," one of the girls taunted as she aimed her phone's camera at me. For all I knew, she was live-streaming this entire incident.

"Maybe she's doing cosplay? Or a movie?" my favorite barista suggested. They gave me a helpless wave of recognition, accompanied by an awkward smile, not knowing what else to do.

"Really? Huh. She's even taller in person."

"You think I can I get a selfie with her?"

I groaned as more people lifted their phones and started snapping photos and taking video.

As if my life wasn't already spiraling into chaos, now I had the added weight of my famous name bearing down on me.

All I wanted in that moment was to crawl into Jack and Chess's arms. When they looked at me, they didn't define me by the worst moments of my life the way everybody else in the world did. My eyes started to sting as I realized the horrible mistake I'd just made.

"Alright, everyone calm down," another officer

intervened, attempting to diffuse the situation. "Put the phones away. Let's get statements from everyone involved and sort this out."

"Statements? For what?" I hissed, my anxiety flaring. "I didn't do anything wrong!"

"Miss, if you don't cooperate, we'll have no choice but to detain you," the first officer warned, her tone firm.

"Detain me? For what?" My voice cracked, unable to comprehend the absurdity of the situation. Instead of enjoying a much-needed break from Wonderland, I was now being accused of assault in my own world.

"Can't you see this is all just a big misunderstanding?" I pleaded, my voice cracking under the weight of humiliation and frustration.

"Miss Darling, have you been using any legal or illegal substances today?" the first officer questioned. His tone suggested he'd already made up his mind about me.

"Of course not!" I snapped, my patience wearing thin. "I'm telling the truth! Look, it's been a long day, and I just want to go home."

"Do you have any health conditions that require medication?"

I folded my arms over my chest.

"I'm not telling you my medical history without a fucking court order! Now, are you gonna arrest me, or can I go home?"

"We need to make sure you're safe," said the

female officer, trying to sound compassionate, but it came off as patronizing.

Out in the parking lot, I saw an ambulance and a few other vehicles pull up. A bunch of paparazzi were suddenly crowding around the windows as the officers met with some EMTs and ushered me into the ambulance.

I only went willingly to get away from all the damn cameras.

Everything after that happened in a rapid-fire blur. I was strapped down onto the stretcher as pieces of my armor were taken off. The EMTs flashed lights in my eyes, took my pulse, took my blood, and asked me what day it was and how long I'd been in Wonderland.

Alice . . . where are you going?

"I don't know, Jack," I said, fighting off tears. "I'm scared!"

The ambulance ride to the mental asylum was a blur of noise and chaos, my mind grasping at straws, searching for some semblance of reason in all of this madness. I knew I sounded insane, but dammit, it was all true!

"Why aren't you calling my lawyer? Can't you see that locking me up won't solve anything?" I implored. The EMTs acted like they had no idea what I was saying. Maybe the words I heard in my head weren't what was coming out of my mouth.

That sometimes happened when I drank too much.

"Alice, try to relax for us, okay?" one of them said, reaching for a radio to fill the silence. I wanted to kick and scream, but I knew it would only make things worse.

When we arrived at the imposing, gray building, my heart sank. It looked like something straight out of a horror film, complete with an eerie fog that clung to the ground. I shivered involuntarily as we walked to the entrance, the heavy iron doors creaking open with a groan.

Once inside, I was escorted to a small, windowless room where a nurse was waiting for me. The harsh fluorescent lights above seemed to accentuate my vulnerability. I could feel their eyes on me, stripping me of any last shred of dignity.

"Take these," the nurse instructed, thrusting a small paper cup filled with pills towards me. One of them was blue.

Blue pills were bad.

"Not until you tell me what they are."

"It's something to calm you down."

I eyed her suspiciously.

"Calm me down? More like drug me into submission," I spat, my voice laced with venom. "Hard pass."

"It's not an option. The powers that be have

determined you're a danger to yourself in your current state."

I stared at her in silence, listening to the buzz of the fluorescent lights and the ticking of the clock on the wall.

Tick . . .

Tock . . .

Tick . . .

Tock . . .

"We can sit here all day," she said, looking bored. "I still get paid the same."

Jack . . . Chess . . . Ransom . . . where are you guys? I wondered. *Callister? Hatter? Can anyone hear me?* I brought my eyes back to the nurse standing in front of me.

"What happens if I refuse?"

"I call in some orderlies to give you an injection." Her eyes were cold and unyielding. "It's your choice. The pill has fewer side effects."

I reluctantly took the cup and tossed the pills into my mouth, feeling them hit the back of my throat like tiny bullets.

"Swallow them," she commanded, handing me a plastic cup of water. The bitter taste of the anti-psychotics filled my mouth as I complied, acutely aware that any sense of control was slipping through my fingers.

"Good girl," she said curtly.

I loved it when Callister said that to me . . . but I hated hearing it from this sour-faced woman who clearly hated her job.

"Alright, now take off your shirt and top and hand them over. You can change into this." She handed me a thin, scratchy hospital gown and a pair of non-slip socks. I hesitated for a moment, my mind racing with memories of Jack's hands roaming over my body, his breath hot against my skin as he whispered dark promises into my ear. I thought about being consumed by him . . . by all of my wicked boys. Even my warm, soft Balenciaga sweatshirt I'd conjured out of thin air was better than this.

But now, in this sterile room, I was at the mercy of strangers.

And I couldn't hear Jack anymore.

"Please," I begged softly, "Can't I have some privacy?"

"Privacy is a luxury you lost when you came here," the nurse replied in a bored tone. As her overworked and underpaid gaze bored into mine, I reluctantly disrobed and put on the hospital gown, feeling utterly exposed and humiliated.

At least the paparazzi couldn't see me like this.

She led me down a dim grey hallway lined with locked doors. My legs were starting to feel wobbly beneath me, the drugs already beginning to take effect. My heart pounded in my chest, each step I took heavy with dread.

"Here we are," she announced, opening the door to a small room that looked more like a prison cell. I glanced inside, my stomach churning at the sight of the stark white walls and floor. I began to feel claus-

trophobic the second the door slammed shut behind
me, the sound echoing through my very bones.

This was now my prison, my purgatory.

Hopelessness and despair coursed through me as
I slid down to the smooth tiled floor, my knees drawn
up to my chest. My stomach was upset.

This was my reality now—trapped in a world that
refused to understand me, with only the memories of
my wicked boys of Wonderland to keep me company.

Being with them had changed me in ways I was
only now beginning to comprehend. I didn't belong
here anymore, in this world that had once seemed so
full of possibility. My heart remained behind, torn
into five pieces and scattered across a land of magic
and danger.

A single tear slid down my cheek as I gazed
around at the mess I'd made of my life. The ache
inside was a physical pain, one that told me I might
never again feel whole.

I'd made my choice, and now I would have to live
with the consequences. Even if I got out of this
asylum, it still meant an eternity of longing for a
world I could never return to.

As the drugs gradually pulled me under, I started
to feel nauseous. One wave after another washed
over me, bathing me in sweat and sickness.

The sudden urge to puke hit me so fast that I
didn't have time to call for someone to let me out. My
stomach lurched and I hurled a thick, nasty, glob of
something awful. The second I saw what came out of
me, I screamed bloody murder.

It was the blue pill, wiggling on the ground as it grew bigger and longer and turned into a glittering fat worm.

And it was inching its way towards the door.

Still screaming my head off, I kicked it against the wall, then nudged it like a slimy hockey puck over to my twin bed. I lifted up the corner, then slammed the leg down on the blue worm as hard as I could.

"Again!" I shouted, imagining all of Jack's relentless training. "Again!" I kept slamming the leg of my bed down until I'd obliterated the worm into a gooey blue smear on the hard tile. Then I gave it a few more slams for good measure.

"Let me out of here!" I screamed, pulling on the doorknob and twisting it, but it was of no use. I started pounding my fists against the door. The tiny window was the size of a postcard—it offered no chance of escape. "Let me out of here! I don't belong here! Please, somebody help me!"

But my cries went unanswered, leaving me alone with the echoes of my own despair. I sank to the floor, my body wracked with sobs as I fought against the rising tide of drug-induced darkness that threatened to consume me.

"Jack," I whispered through the haze of tears and panic, clinging to the memory of his voice like a lifeline. "If you can hear me . . . please . . . do whatever you have to do to get me out of here."

Silence.

So much silence.

I groaned, then shut my eyes, using my imagina-

273

tion to picture him and Chess, Ransom and Hatter and Callister, all gathered in the courtyard. I thought of them and only them, as hard as I could, fighting the unconsciousness of sleep.

Just before I drifted away, I heard the most beautiful sound.

Hold on, Alice . . .

We're coming to get you.

Pssst . . .
I need your opinion. Got a sec?

Leaving reviews is one of the most kickass ways to support authors. You're also helping other readers decide if our books are right for them. If you have a minute, I'd LOVE a review from you!

Review Jack of Diamonds on Amazon

Review Jack of Diamonds on Goodreads

Thanks so much!

Jekka

JEKKA'S WILDE ONES

Desperate for more?

Join Jekka's Wilde Ones!

Get immediate access to Jekka's private Facebook group, character art, the spiciest new Fantasy & PNR books, and be notified of new releases before anyone else.

Become a Wilde One at jekkawilde.com/ newsletter

ABOUT THE AUTHOR

Jekka Wilde (aka the Duchess of Depravity) reigns supreme in her frostbitten kingdom in the northern US, where she's practically *forced* to write steamy stories to stay warm.

A self-proclaimed caffeine aficionado, she can often be found snuggled under a blanket fortress, sipping a matcha latte that's almost as hot as the scorching scenes in her books.

In a house that's part library, part shoe warehouse, Jekka's motto in life and literature is 'Why Choose?'— a philosophy that's evident in every romance she writes. The only thing filthier than her humor is the plot.

If you're looking for sweet romance, keep walking. But if you're ready for a wild, witty, and wicked ride, congratulations!

You've just found your new favorite author.

Printed in the USA
CPSIA information can be obtained
at www.ICGtesting.com
LVHW040845280724
786708LV00002B/27